T AND A
HE UNIV

CU00841606

T.A.S.C. LIBRARY LEEDS

095356 2

THE GREEN BOUGH OF LIBERTY

By the same author

STORM SURGE
QUINTIN'S MAN
THE MISSING GERMAN
LANDSLIP
THE SPECTRUM
THE FERRYMAN
RISKS
THE EXETER BLITZ
THE HOUSE THAT MOVED
IN THE TENT
SILENCE

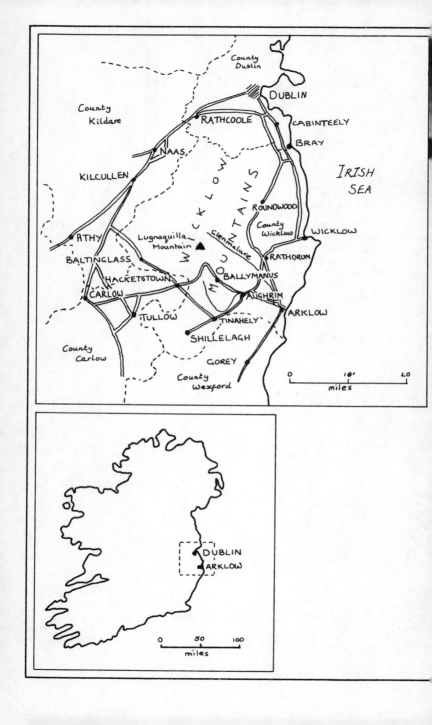

David Rees

THE GREEN BOUGH OF LIBERTY

LONDON : DENNIS DOBSON

© *Copyright 1979 by David Rees*
All rights reserved

For my cousin Michael

J
823

95356

First published in Great Britain 1979 by
Dobson Books Ltd., 80 Kensington Church Street, London W.8

Photoset in Great Britain by
Photobooks (Bristol) Ltd.,
28/30 Midland Road, St. Philips,
Bristol
Printed and bound in Great Britain by
William Clowes (Beccles) Limited, Beccles and London

ISBN 0 234 72187 1

A wet winter, a dry spring,
A bloody summer, and no King.
            —ancient prophecy for the year 1798

She's the most distressful country that ever yet was seen
            —old Irish street ballad

The tree of liberty must be refreshed from time to time
with the blood of patriots and tyrants. It is its natural
manure.
            —Thomas Jefferson

CHAPTER ONE

ARKLOW

No more peaceful scene in the whole county of Wicklow could be imagined, Ned Byrne thought. He was tired from the day's work on the farm, a pleasant physical tiredness that had come mainly from the job of cutting down brambles and saplings, clearing ferns and bushes from a piece of waste land that Garret had decided should come under the plough. It would in time make a field of reasonable size, Garret said; they would need it for the cattle: the pasture was already being grazed to the maximum it could tolerate.

Ned, at ease in the armchair in front of the fire and sleepy with the heat, stretched and yawned. His sister Fanny had certainly cooked them a good dinner; they did not have roast chicken every day of the week. Now, the meal over and the dishes cleared away, the family was in the drawing room, happily engaged in their usual evening pastimes. Garret was sitting behind his desk, reading; it was sure to be a book on agriculture, Ned decided. Garret, the eldest of the three brothers and the owner of Ballymanus, was all for the latest new methods of farming; he was constantly reading about how to obtain more milk from the cows, or how to improve on the quantity of oats and turnips and cabbages in his fields. Ned smiled as he watched his brother frown, reading glasses perched on the end of his nose; Garret was

7

always an enthusiast, whether it was for the Ballymanus estate, or politics: the Wicklow leaders of the Society of United Irishmen sometimes met in this drawing room and plotted the downfall of the English government in Ireland. Ned was excluded from these meetings, somewhat to his annoyance. The youngest of the family he might well be, but he was eighteen and thought he should be treated as an adult and share his brothers' confidences.

Fanny was sitting on the sofa and talking to Garret's wife, Mary. Women's chatter in polite formal language, an imitation of Dublin society speech: Ned listened, and wondered how it was they could be so interested in whether tamboured muslin was more fetching than the spotted variety.

'Oh, from a box in a Dublin theatre,' Mary said, 'one can see such a collection of gowns as could satisfy any woman's taste!'

'Is that so?' Fanny asked, needle poised to make the next stitch. 'I have not often had the good fortune to visit a Dublin theatre, buried as we are in the country.' She was making a little white jacket for her nephew, Dermot. She doted on the child, who was not yet a year old: the first of the new generation, she often said proudly, the first-born of the first-born, Garret's and Mary's son.

'I have to admit,' Mary said, 'that I do miss the theatre and all the bustle of city life. One cannot help it, I suppose.' She concentrated on her stitches; she too was sewing, a cap for Dermot to match the jacket Fanny was creating. 'Not that I would change this place for the whole world! I love my dear husband, and Ballymanus is the most beautiful of houses. Yes . . . I have great good fortune to be mistress of Ballymanus.'

Fanny glanced at her in surprise. Her sister-in-law was, of

8

course, the mistress of the house, but the family sometimes forgot that she was. Fanny had been in charge of all the household duties since her parents had died, and when Garret brought his young wife home from Dublin, that arrangement had continued. Mary seemed to have no wish to take over the running of things, and Fanny had no mind to be displaced from the position she had happily occupied for some years. 'This design is too intricate,' she said, holding up the jacket for Mary to inspect. 'I think perhaps I should have chosen a plainer pattern.'

'Oh no,' Mary answered. 'It will suit very well.'

'Do you think so?'

'To be sure! Why, he will look more regal in that than Lord Camden himself.'

Ned, bored with the conversation, stood up and went over to the table at the other end of the room where his grandfather was peering through a magnifying glass at some ancient documents and muttering to himself. 'Leave all that rubbish, you old fool,' he said. 'Come and play a game of chess with me.'

'Chess you want, is it?' Grandfather asked.

'And a wager on the game. Sixpence.'

The old man could not resist the idea of a bet; he shuffled his documents together and said 'Well, first let me light my pipe.' This operation took some time, but when he had succeeded in manufacturing a cloud of smoke sufficiently dense, he tipped the pieces on to the board, and said 'This is the best of games. Two armies of equal strength, poised for battle.'

'So you always say, Grandfather.'

'England against Ireland. Who is to be which? Shall we toss a coin?'

Garret looked up from his reading. 'Don't trust him, Ned.

His money has the same image on both sides; there's no picture of the King.'

Grandfather protested. 'How can you talk such nonsense, Garret!'

'Easily enough.'

'It's entirely untrue!' But whatever the truth of it, Grandfather won the toss, and Ned, with the black pieces, was the British army. 'When you go for a soldier, Ned, make sure it is not as one of the King's men.' He pushed his queen's pawn forward, an unusual opening for him.

'Of course I shan't!' Ned answered, trying to remember the standard reply to white's opening gambit. 'I shall be one of the wild geese.'

'Ah, the wild geese! The Irishmen of the French army! Well, Napoleon will find you a good soldier I'm thinking.' Garret had inherited the farm, so it was impossible for Ned or for Billy, the middle brother, to stay at Ballymanus for ever. Billy, perhaps, would become a priest. He hadn't made up his mind about it yet; it was a big decision to take: one on which there would be no going back. While he was thinking it over, he, too, helped on the farm, and joined Garret in his clandestine political talk with the United Irishmen. Ned, in his wish to join the French army, was following a course that the younger sons of the Irish gentry often followed: there was little hope of advancement for them in their own country, oppressed and down-trodden under British rule.

'Where is Billy?' Ned asked.

'In his room.' Grandfather removed a pawn Ned had left unguarded. 'You see? Ireland already has the upper hand. Ned . . . you may have a chance to fight somewhat earlier than you imagine.'

He looked up, startled. 'What do you mean?' It had always been understood that he would not leave home until

10

he was at least twenty-one. And, at the moment, he certainly did not want to go; he was becoming more than vaguely interested in a distant cousin, Ellen Kennedy, who lived with her mother in a cottage about a mile away. She was the prettiest girl he had ever seen.

'Do you not know the old prophecy for Ireland for this year, 1798?'

'Yes. A wet winter, a dry spring, a bloody summer, and no King.'

'The winter was wet and the spring was dry. It's nearly summer now: April. All the blossom and scents . . . things growing, plots hatching. Just think on.'

'Why, what have you heard?' Ned moved his queen to threaten one of Grandfather's bishops.

'Ssh.' The old man laid a finger against the left side of his nose. 'Secrecy is a most important lesson to master. I know what I know.'

Ned followed the direction of the old man's stare. 'What? Garret? I never take his United Irishmen seriously at all. A nest of stage conspirators, all cloak and dagger stuff; quite harmless. Are they up to something?'

'You'll see.'

'It's about time they let me become party to their mysteries. It's not right!'

Grandfather, thinking several moves ahead, allowed his bishop to be swept off the board by the black queen, and from the ensuing slaughter, which decimated most of the pawns and all of the knights, he emerged a piece up: Ned had inadvertently lost a rook.

They surveyed the battlefield in silence for some time. 'I surrender,' Ned said eventually. 'I surely cannot win with only one castle. Here's your sixpence, you old rogue.'

Grandfather celebrated his victory with a sigh. 'You

11

might still have won, Ned. You give in too easily.' He pocketed the coin; Ned returned to the armchair and gazed into the fire.

Fanny stood up and announced that she would make tea for everybody. As she was leaving the room, Billy came in. 'Daydreaming is it, Little Ned?' he inquired with a laugh. 'Pictures in the flames?' Ned looked at him: Billy was dressed to go out.

'Don't call me by that absurd nickname,' he said, crossly. 'It's foolish, and I taller than any of you.'

Billy smiled. 'Eighteen years and six feet of man already! A power of fine women will want to know you. How will you deal with that?'

'As successfully and as often as six feet of man is able to.' If Fanny were present, Ned thought, she would object to such words: Ned! Language! she would say. He laughed to himself; he enjoyed teasing his sister.

'That sounds not quite moral,' Billy said.

'I daresay wild geese are in the habit of sowing wild oats.'

Billy stopped smiling. It was not possible to tease him; he took everything too seriously. 'With wild consequences, no doubt,' he said.

'Oh . . . I'll worry about that after. I was only giving you a light answer, Billy. To a light question. Why are you dressed up? Where are you going?'

'Out.'

'That is not a light answer. It's no answer at all.'

'Quite true,' Billy said, and walked away. He leaned over the desk and spoke to Garret, so low and so close to his ear that Ned could not make out a single word. Garret took off his glasses, nodded, and asked a few questions. The replies appeared to satisfy him, for he nodded again, and said, loud enough for all to hear, 'Good luck.'

12

Billy in his smartest clothes looked very handsome, Ned thought. Not that any of the four of them were ugly—except for the family nose. The long Roman nose of the Byrnes; it was quite a joke amongst them. It was invariably passed on from one generation to the next; Billy's was no different from Grandfather's. Their hair colouring was the same too, jet black, but Ned's curled, and so did Fanny's, though hers was not natural: to put her in the fashion the hairdresser had had to provide something that Ned had been born with. Their faces, the build of their bodies, though obviously the work of the same parents, showed marked differences, reflected character. Garret, the gentleman farmer, tall, with an air of authority: his eyes could blaze and flash, not from bad temper but single-mindedness, the need to do everything well down to the smallest detail. Billy's eyes were milder, occasionally reproachful, but always showing a softer disposition, that of an altruistic man, essentially kind and unselfish. A vulnerable person, it occurred to Ned, one who needed protection. He was very fond of Billy, and admired him; perhaps, he sometimes thought, because the recesses of Billy's mind were very hard to penetrate. Fanny . . . well, Fanny was no raving beauty though attractive enough, but she never took much notice of the opposite sex despite her interest in fashions and hair-styles. A simple domesticated girl, in Ned's opinion.

And himself? In body the strongest of the three brothers. Garret and Billy liked books, but Ned went no further for his satisfactions than the labour of the farm and physical pursuits, hunting, shooting, walking for miles in the mountains. He was a less complicated person than the other two, more animal; and unlike Billy he was fond of the company of women.

And now, he thought, that is enough intellectual exercise

for one day, summing up the family characters: he went to sit on the sofa beside Mary, pass her the tea and make a fuss of her in order that he could be fussed in turn. 'It's a pleasure to be an uncle,' he said. 'It makes one feel adult. As if the years between being the size of Dermot and the size of being me have been a long time.'

'People grow up quickly enough,' she said, 'but to those who are doing the growing it can seem long. And hard.'

'Quite so.'

'And . . . you think you have finished the growing season?' She tried to suppress a smile, but he noticed, and decided to tread warily, not wanting to be laughed at.

'I doubt if one ever finishes that,' he said, choosing his words. 'But one . . . *I* . . . feel I've reached a stage. I don't know where. Some ledge part way up the hill.'

'And you want to spread your wings and fly away.'

'Wild geese again?'

'I didn't say where you should fly. I was thinking of Ellen.'

'Ah. Ellen.'

She laughed, not mockingly, and said 'Maybe that's your next stage.'

'I can't think of her as a stage, as something you stop at for a while in order to move on.'

Mary settled herself more comfortably on the sofa and sipped her tea. 'Men should know a great many women before they settle on one in particular. I would not go into a Dublin shop and buy a hat without first trying all on display to see how they suit.'

He looked round. 'I'm glad my sister is not in earshot,' he said. Fanny was with Garret, both of them looking at pictures in a book, and laughing at something Grandfather had just said.

14

'Why?' Mary asked.

'She wouldn't approve. Of the idea of girls being like hats to try on.'

'Ah, you'd be surprised what she and I have to say to each other at times!'

'Would I?' The thought of Mary and Fanny discussing men in their private conversations had not occurred to Ned. 'Tell me.'

'Certainly not!'

'Maybe I should.'

'Maybe you should what?'

'Try on the hats.' He sighed. 'But it isn't at all like that, is it?'

'Meaning you're in love with Ellen?'

'Am I? I don't know. At least . . . I'm not going to admit it.'

She laughed, and stood up. 'All you can do is find out for yourself. I must go upstairs and see to Dermot.'

'I didn't hear him.'

'No. But you weren't listening for him and I was.' She left the room. Billy had also gone: strange, Ned thought, that he had slipped out so quietly and unnoticed, not even saying good-bye. What was he up to? Not visiting a young woman, that was certain. Which, Ned supposed, was quite appropriate for a man who was thinking of being ordained as a priest.

'Fanny,' he said, 'sister dear! Come and talk to your little brother, your Little Ned.'

'No, no,' she answered. 'I have work to do in the kitchen, a cake to bake.'

'At this hour of the night?'

'Why not? You won't be considering what hour of the day it is when you want to eat it.'

15

He could not interrupt Grandfather again; the old man was immersed once more in his documents. Grandfather, or Garret Byrne the Elder, as some of his friends called him, spent much of his time sorting through family papers, wills, old deeds, old letters. He was sure the family would one day need to have them in order; the English would try to trick the Byrnes out of their inheritance. Had they not already done so in the past, with great success? Two hundred, three hundred years ago the Byrnes had been Lords of Ranelagh, the greatest family in Wicklow, owners of vast tracts of land, almost the whole county. Now look at them! His grandchildren scorned his whims, and he would counter their frivolity with long stories of how much worse their life would have been only fifty years previously, when the Penal Laws were carried out with much greater rigour than they were now. Fifty years ago, an Irish Catholic was not allowed to follow any respectable trade or profession, to vote or to sit on a jury; he couldn't be educated in a school or buy land. If he inherited land, it was split equally between him and his brothers: that, more than anything else, had impoverished the people. The Byrnes had survived only because the younger brothers had always left the country, going to Rome for a priest, or joining foreign armies in France or America. Why, in those days a Catholic wasn't even allowed to own a gun or a horse! What on earth would Garret and Billy and Ned do without a gun or a horse?

No, Ned thought, a sermon on those lines would be his only reward if he interrupted the old man. You could tell easily enough when it was possible and when it was not possible to disturb Grandfather; if the magnifying glass was held as close to the paper as it was now, or if the mutterings were a constant stream of incoherent noises instead of the occasional word or grunt, then it was not a good moment.

16

Grandfather was now muttering away in a state of high excitement. Ned went and stood behind Garret, leaning against the window. 'Where's Billy gone?' he asked.

Garret shut his book with a bang—Thomas Coke, Ned observed; a treatise on the rotation of crops in Norfolk—and turned his chair round so that he was facing his youngest brother. 'To Arklow,' he said.

'To Arklow! At this time of night! It's miles away!'

'He's not returning till tomorrow morning. He'll be stopping with friends.'

'But . . . why?'

Garret did not answer immediately, but looked hard at Ned for some moments. What revelation was coming, Ned asked himself. Surely something of importance. Was he, after all this time, to be made privy to the secrets of the United Irishmen? 'He has gone to join the Wicklow Yeomen Cavalry,' Garret said.

'What!!' Ned was thunderstruck. 'Billy has gone for a soldier! And in a *British* regiment! What is this? What is going on?'

'He thinks the government troops should be infiltrated by United spies and sympathisers. I must admit . . . I'm not myself quite happy about the idea.'

'Billy for a soldier!' Ned exclaimed again. 'It's preposterous! He hasn't the bearing, the wish, the . . . the first notion! He'll be laughed out of the barracks! Can you see him drilling, or shouldering a musket? You should have sent me! Why don't you trust *me*?'

'I do trust you, Ned.' Garret was patient, impassive almost, as he listened to Ned's outburst. He knew, of course, that it was only to be expected.

Ned had a lot more to say about trust and loyalty, about which member of the family was supposed to be the priest

17

and which the soldier, about feeling betrayed and being unfairly kept out of things; when he had exhausted his fit of ill-temper, he paused for a moment, then asked 'Does Fanny know of this?'

'Not yet,' Garret answered. 'She thinks Billy has gone to visit a sick friend.'

'It's time you told me everything, Garret!'

'Maybe it is. Or some of it. Well, first of all, a history lesson.'

'I don't want a history lesson!'

'You are going to have one whether you like it or not! Now draw up a chair and help yourself to a glass of whiskey, or light a pipe if you wish.' Ned did all three, and when he was settled, Garret said 'The Society of United Irishmen was formed in 1791 by Wolfe Tone.'

'I know that,' Ned interrupted, puffing angrily on his pipe. 'I'm not a child!'

'Very well. And so you know, I imagine, that it originally consisted of Protestants, that it started in Ulster, that Catholics soon joined it, that their aims were to secure some kind of parliamentary reform, that—'

'Yes, yes, yes! I also know that in recent years it's been more interested in overthrowing the government by force, that it wants to found an independent Irish republic modelled on the Directoire, and that it was deeply involved with the French two years ago when Admiral Hoche's fleet was destroyed in that storm off Bantry. I suppose they would have achieved something if the French had landed. Yes . . . I agree with their aims; of course I do: I just don't think it's very probable that they'll succeed, that's all. I imagine there are too many people who like the sound of their own voices, and spout a lot of weird ideas that are hopelessly impractical. Typically Irish, in fact.'

18

'You know more than I thought.'

'I may be a bit dumb where books are concerned, but I'm not blind! Or deaf, for that matter.'

'No indeed. Books . . . it might do some of our supporters a power of good if they read fewer books. Too many ideas circulate based on the crazier theories of the French Revolution. The point is, the time draws near. There *is* to be an armed insurrection against the government.'

Ned was silent. At long last Garret was treating him as an equal! 'When?'

'Soon. Very soon. I don't know the exact date; that has still to be decided. The leaders are meeting in a few days' time at Oliver Bond's house in Dublin; we shall know after that. I shan't be there; I'm not one of the inner council, the National Directory as it is called. I'm merely a member of the Leinster Directory, and so is Billy.'

'Why are you telling me all this? Do I have a part to play?'

'Yes, you do.'

'What is it?'

'I'm not saying just now. You must wait and see.'

'No! Tell me now!'

'I will not!!' Garret spoke so loudly and authoritatively that not only did Ned realise that there was nothing to be gained from pressing the point, but Grandfather, who had worked blithely on through Ned's impassioned words without hearing a single one of them, looked up and peered distractedly round the room.

Eventually he focused on Garret and said 'What is the matter? Is Little Ned being troublesome? I don't know, Garret; you're twenty-six and married, the master of Ballymanus, and you will let yourself be over-ridden by a chit of eighteen! You can still tan his arse.'

19

'Chit! Tan my arse!' Ned exploded with laughter. 'Why, I could bend him in two!'

'Twenty-six,' Garret repeated. 'Billy is twenty-three and Fanny twenty-one.' He looked worried. 'They're not old enough I'm thinking for what is to happen. They have little experience of life.'

'What about me?' Ned asked. 'I'm even younger.'

'Oh, you! You know nothing at all. But you're as hard as nails! You're a born survivor.'

'Why . . . thank you, Garret.' Ned felt absurdly pleased. 'That's one of the nicest things you have ever said to me.'

Garret laughed and re-opened his book. The discussion was closed.

Ned, his mind teeming with the implications of what he had heard, felt he could not remain indoors. The room was insufferably hot; why did they need fires in late April? Presumably for Grandfather, who was old and his blood thin, and the baby Dermot: Mary did fuss excessively over the child's state of health. But the heat almost asphyxiated everyone else. He left the house and walked down the drive. The night was deliciously cool, full of flower scents drifting on the breeze, full of the promise of summer, of warm days when he could swim or wander in the fields with Ellen. Yes, Ellen: he hadn't seen her since yesterday, for she had been to Aughrim with her mother; but by now they would surely have arrived back home. He would go down to the cottage and see. The very idea of her gave him a shiver of excitement, another kind of promise.

Maybe it was a pity, he thought, that he knew less of books than his brothers did. None of the three had received any formal education; there were no schools Catholics could attend in this mountainous, thinly populated part of Wicklow. Their father had hired tutors who had taught them at

20

home. So they all spoke French, could construe their Latin, and they had read Shakespeare. No, he was not an illiterate; Ellen would not be much interested in him if his entire conversation was of pigs and sheep and the price of oats. He had learned his Bible too, and knew the words of the Mass, but he had not been tutored in his religion at home. He had attended the hedgerow school: a collection of children gathered together by the priest down near the cross-roads on the way to Aughrim. There he had been taught his commandments and his catechism. Ned was always one of the strong lads stationed on the edges of this group; he was supposed to keep an eye open for Protestant neighbours who might report Father Dolan to the authorities or try to break things up by using some kind of violence. Maybe it was because of being on the fringe of it, and finding his job as watchman rather exciting, that he had taken in less than Billy had. Ned believed in God, went to Mass when it was possible, and said his prayers, but he didn't think much about it. Billy thought about it all the time.

What does it matter, he said to himself; in his own way he was just as good a man as Billy. He had never done anything terribly wrong like stealing or fornication or murder. His sins were the same as those of other boys: disobedience, lying when necessary for his own safety, impure thoughts about girls. Sexual longings had been troublesome for some years now; he had even once gone to the lengths of telling Billy, asking his brother how he managed to put such promptings out of his mind. 'You fight against them,' Billy said. 'Prayer is a very powerful weapon.' But Ned must have looked quite bewildered, for Billy relented, saying 'Ah well, I don't suppose the good Lord will send you to eternal damnation for a few sweet dreams.' And did Billy have such dreams, Ned inquired. 'Of course,' was the answer, rather

21

brusque and off-hand. Billy had revealed something that he didn't, perhaps, care to show.

Nowadays Ned's desires centred on Ellen, but, tempted though he may have been, he had not tried to put any of them into practice. He would never do such a thing, no, not till he was married. How long would it be before he could even think of marrying? Years and years! He, without a penny to his name, destined to leave Ireland, to fight in a foreign army! What unfair accident had made him a younger son? Why couldn't he have inherited Ballymanus instead of Garret? If he was the eldest son he could marry Ellen tomorrow; well, maybe not tomorrow, for he would have to ask her mother's permission and he was not on the best of terms with Mrs Kennedy. She did not like to see her daughter becoming involved with a boy of eighteen, one of the wild geese to be. A wild gosling, in fact. She would doubtless want Ellen married off to a land-owner like Garret. Still, he wasn't afraid of Mrs Kennedy. He arrived at the cottage and knocked on the door.

'Tell us, Mr Byrne, why should an Irish gentleman such as yourself wish to join the regiment?' The recruiting officer looked through some papers on his desk. 'Isn't it more commonly the custom of you people to seek . . . ah . . . how shall I put it? Employment abroad?'

The British army captain was no fool, Billy realized. What had seemed at the outset a relatively simple task was turning into something like a nightmare. Under the penetrating gaze of the three red-coated soldiers he felt stripped, no longer honest plain Billy Byrne of Ballymanus, but a shifty and evasive creature, an object of suspicion. 'I do not want to go abroad,' he said. 'I would prefer to stay here and protect my own countrymen.'

'Protect them from whom?' the captain asked.

'Why . . . from whoever may disturb the peace.' Silence greeted this; Billy felt obliged to continue. 'Rumours abound of conspiracies and schemes . . . the French may try another invasion.' He paused, licking his lips nervously. He could feel sweat on his brow. 'There are surely other Irish Catholics who join the British army, who even hold commissions in regiments stationed in this country. I have heard of such people; indeed I know a few, but . . . to be quite open . . . I did not imagine they were subject to an examination of this sort.'

'Times have changed,' the captain said. 'We are all of us aware, as I'm sure you are too, that rebellion is plotted against the Crown. You are not so out of the way in rural Wicklow that you have not at least heard of the Society of United Irishmen. Of Wolfe Tone and Lord Edward Fitzgerald.'

'Of course I've heard of them. Who has not?'

'What do you think of their ideas?'

How should he answer such a question? With a down-right lie, of course, and an unflinching expression, but it was not easy for Billy to lie. Garret would be able to, and carry it off successfully, even though he might dislike himself for doing so; Ned would find it even easier than Garret: Ned would speak up without the slightest qualm, without his conscience being at all troubled, knowing instinctively that a man usually says anything expedient to get himself out of a tight corner. 'I think nothing of their ideas,' he said at last.

The two soldiers on either side of the captain, recruiting sergeants with fierce faces and bristling moustaches, glanced at one another as if to say this man is not what he seems; in a moment all will be revealed. The captain, who was clean-shaven, and whose manner was inquisitorial rather than military, leaned forward. 'Speak plainly,' he said. 'Do you disagree with their aims? Or you haven't the time, or the interest, or perhaps the ability to understand what these people are about?'

'They are impetuous and extreme,' Billy answered. It was near enough to the truth for him to be able to say it.

'You haven't answered the question.'

'I . . . do not agree with their aims.' He loathed himself for those words; they were a direct lie. And the tone of voice in which he spoke, reluctant and quiet, would, he felt certain, betray his real position.

'You see, Mr Byrne . . . it does not escape us that it may well be the policy of the United people to try and infiltrate our ranks. Oh yes, I'm sure they have their spies in Dublin Castle who report to their leaders what the government thinks and says, what contingencies it will have prepared in the event of revolution; just as the government will doubtless have planted informers in United circles. Success frequently hangs on men's extraordinary willingness to betray their country for money. And it is an easy step to move from the political to the military.' He paused; his manner changed: now he was being confidential. 'In other words, and this is the reasoning for our hard questioning, we fear we may have recruited United symphathizers among our soldiers. They could be very destructive to us, not only as spies, but as saboteurs, arms-runners, spreaders of discontent among impressed men. You see our problem.'

Billy did see their problem: it had been his idea in the first place to weaken the Yeomen Cavalry in just this manner. But the regiment was one step ahead of him, knowing his plans even before he had a chance to put them into practice. What did it mean? That there was a government spy in the

24

Leinster Directory? Yes, of course there were spies in the Leinster Directory, but this particular spy, if he existed, was more locally placed than that; he must be one of the United men of the immediate neighbourhood, one who had possibly even been entertained as a guest at Ballymanus.

'Well, what shall we do about it?' The captain sounded more genial, more business-like, as if he had come to a decision. 'On the face of it you are exactly the kind of man we need. A gentleman of ancient family and a Catholic; obviously a person of influence, someone whose example would persuade others to like action. But . . . please forgive us . . . that is all the more reason to take care.' He took a sheet of paper from the bottom of the pile in front of him. 'So we shall give you a simple test.'

'A test?'

The captain smiled. 'We call it the Test Oath.' He passed the paper to Billy and said 'Read it to yourself, then repeat the words aloud, holding the Good Book in your right hand.' He pointed to the Bible, which was lying on the desk in front of him.

It would be impossible, absolutely out of the question, Billy thought as he read through what was written on the paper, to utter these words aloud. It would be perjuring his very soul. 'I'—then there was a blank space for him to say his full name—'do, in the presence of my neighbours, solemnly swear by the contents of this book containing the Holy Gospels of Christ that I have not joined, nor in any manner entered into any society or association of persons styling themselves "United Irishmen" or any other seditious society whatsoever, or taken any oath to keep the secrets of any such society, or taken any oath to the prejudice of His Majesty King George the Third, or contrary to the existing laws or constitution of this Kingdom of Ireland; and all this I

25

do freely and voluntarily swear, without any mental evasion or secret reservation whatsoever. So help me God.'

So help him God if he said all that with his hand on the Bible! Yes, he could say with an easy conscience that he had not taken any oaths prejudicial to the King, for that was the truth; but to swear on the Holy Gospels of Christ that he was not a member of the United Irishmen . . . he would never be able to live with himself.

He was conscious of three pairs of eyes watching him intently; the captain was even smiling. 'I cannot swear to this,' he said at last.

The captain took the paper from him. 'Why not?'

'My . . . my neighbours are not present.'

It was a foolish answer, indeed a childish one; the soldiers laughed, and, Billy felt, it deserved no other response. 'Come, come!' said the sergeant nearest to him. 'We will stand in for your neighbours. You wish to be precise, but we are all neighbours in the sight of God.'

'It will not do!'

'It seems quite a simple matter to me,' the captain said.

'I know not . . . whether I may know United men . . . whether it be considered I have associated with such persons . . . It will not do!'

'It's not a crime,' the captain pointed out, 'to share the beliefs of the United Irishmen. Not even a crime to belong to their organisation. Yet.' He picked up the letter Billy had written applying to join the regiment, and tore it to pieces. 'We find you are not a suitable person, Mr Byrne, to serve in His Majesty's armed forces.' He stood up, and showed Billy to the door. 'Where are you staying tonight?'

'With friends, here in town.'

'Be careful, Mr Byrne. From now on you should consider yourself a marked man.'

26

Billy decided not to stay overnight; it might well be
dangerous. He rode home in the dark, as fast as he possibly
could. What a fool he must have seemed to the recruiting
officer! Child-like and simple-minded: any other spy would
have sworn the oath cheerfully, without a flicker of
conscience. All he had done was to show them where his
sympathies lay, and he had gained nothing by doing so. So
idiotic he must have appeared to be that the captain might
well be genuinely puzzled. At the very least he would think
these Irish were ignorant bog-trotters, transparent and
stupid. Well, let him think so. Billy, you are not suited for
these matters, he told himself; you are not made to be a
soldier, an informer, or a politician. The Church was where
he belonged. And were it not for the fact that the best
opportunity for centuries—perhaps ever—had arisen to
help free his country from the chains of slavery, he might
even now be on a ship bound for Rome. It was a cruel
dilemma, but he could not leave now, could not abandon his
brothers and his sister when they were about to be plunged
into what might be the most exciting chapter of the entire
history of Ireland.

What would Garret say of his failure? That he had turned
a promising situation into one which threatened the whole
family's safety; Ned—he knew Garret meant, while he was
away in Arklow, to let Ned into some of their intentions—
would go further and say he was a mad crazy idiot who was
a millstone round the neck of the whole enterprise. And
who could blame his young brother for thinking so? It was
true.

It was very late when he arrived at Ballymanus; the house
was in darkness. He crept quietly up to his room, hoping he
would not disturb anyone. On the table beside his bed was a
crucifix. He knelt down and prayed: 'O Thou that hearest

prayer, unto Thee all flesh shall come. Iniquities prevail against me: as for our transgressions, Thou shalt purge them away. Blessed is the man whom Thou choosest, and causest to approach unto Thee that he may dwell in Thy courts: we shall be satisfied with the goodness of Thy house, even of Thy holy temple. By terrible things in righteousness wilt Thou answer us, O God of our salvation.'

He lay in bed, reading the Book of Proverbs by the light of a candle; a verse in the twelfth chapter he told himself he should always keep in mind: 'A prudent man concealeth knowledge, but the heart of fools proclaimeth foolishness.'

He felt calmer, but his sleep was interrupted by dreams of red-coat soldiers, of massacres, of Ned dying in agony, a pike thrust through his stomach.

Irish loyalists through rebel eyes—"Captn. Swayne Pitch Capping the People of Prosperous."

CHAPTER TWO

SHILLELAGH

Ned leaned on the gate. The field sloped down towards the valley, where the early morning mist was drifting up from the trees, revealing the cottage where Ellen lived. There were glimpses of the road. He could hear a horse galloping, far off, but he could not see it. It would be another fine April morning later.

Billy was standing in the doorway of the house. 'What are you doing, Little Ned?' he called. 'No work today, is it?'

'I'm listening to that horse.' Billy crossed the yard and leaned on the gate, beside him. 'What stranger are we expecting now?' Ned asked.

'Perhaps it is a man for Garret.' Billy looked away, and Ned knew that the stranger was probably expected. It was unpleasant of his brothers to continue to be so secretive after Garret had confided in him.

'Don't call me Little Ned!' He pushed at the gate in some irritation. 'And it's you who should be out of things, after your triumph at Arklow. Not me.'

'I know. I could kick myself every time I think of it. However . . . no harm has come of it yet, though each time I hear a horse I wonder if it is someone coming to take me into custody. Why'—he broke off as the horse and his rider emerged from the mist—'It's Cornelius Sinnott.'

31

The horse slowed as it made its way up the steep narrow lane that led off the Aughrim road. They could see the man's face and hat from time to time through the gaps in the hedge. As the lane evened out the horse's pace quickened; it took at one leap the fence that marked the boundary of the Ballymanus lands, and galloped up to the house, the rider cursing its slowness. He jumped down, tied the horse to a ring in the wall, and dashed inside without waiting for an answer to his knock. His clothes were wet and very muddy.

'Cornelius Sinnott,' Ned repeated. 'A strange name. Who is he?'

'A draper from Wicklow.' Billy went back to the house, but Ned stayed where he was, thinking his presence would not be welcome. He picked up a stone and made to throw it at the door, but changed his mind and skimmed it into the field. He whistled, and a black spaniel dashed across the yard to him, delighted to be noticed. He set off down the drive, the dog sniffing at his heels, but he stopped when he saw Ellen and her mother in the distance. In the past few days Mrs Kennedy seemed to be even more bad-tempered than usual. He climbed over a stile and disappeared into the copse on the south side of the farmhouse, the dog following.

'All the leaders taken at Bond's! Sheares, Thomas Emmet, all of them in prison! And my cousin, William Michael Byrne!' Garret got up from behind his desk, wringing his hands in agitation. He looked pale and his cheeks were hollow; his eyes were restless, straying from one thing to another but seeing nothing. There had been only bad news now for days, and, in consequence, he had hardly slept. 'For the love of God what are we to do?' he asked. 'You surely brought some messages?'

'No sir. So sudden, with no kind of warning—'

32

'Was it?' He paused, and exchanged glances with Billy, who was standing in front of the fire, warming himself. Billy said nothing, but inclined his head towards the door, as if to suggest that Mr Sinnott's usefulness was ended.

'There's nothing more?' Garret asked. 'No? Come to the kitchen then, Mr Sinnott, and my sister will find you something to eat. You must be dirty and hungry, and the roads full of mud.' Garret led him out, and Billy could hear voices in the kitchen raised in argument: Fanny and Mrs Kennedy.

Garret returned. He looked a little more decisive now that he understood the full impact of the news he had heard.

'The worst that could happen *has* happened,' he said to Billy. 'Dublin Castle has planted a spy among us, but I can't even guess who it can be. Reynolds? He didn't come to the meeting at Bond's. Maybe one of those who were arrested? It could be; that would seem like a very good trick. One thing is clear; we can't wait a moment longer. We must start at once.'

Billy looked at his finger-nails, trying to hide his surprise. 'We've always said that a rising is doomed to failure without the French standing by us. At each and every meeting that point has been hammered home, or we'd have lost long ago to the Dantons and Robespierres.'

'We can never wait for them now.' Garret peered out of the window at the monkey-puzzle trees in front of the house. They were a beautiful sight, none like them in all Wicklow. 'They'll still be here when we come back.'

'What?'

'The trees.' He shook his head. 'What was I saying? Napoleon is not much concerned with Ireland. We must start it, and end it, alone.'

'Not much concerned?'

'Oh yes, he might say that he is, but think of the distance! How can he supply all his men? He can't just sail past Howth Head into Kingstown Harbour. A landing would have to be on the west coast, in some wild remote place, Tralee perhaps or Bantry again. How far is it from Paris to Dublin, passing through Bantry? Well, there you are.'

'What do we do then?'

'We raise up every man and lad over eighteen, every fellow in the district who can handle a pike. We only have to tell them it's now. They know what to do. We should meet, I think, at Shillelagh in a week's time. And one further thing, Billy. We must tell the other leaders in Aughrim and Tinahely. With Sinnott back in Wicklow tonight, we have to, and we'll find them in a great haste to act as we are.'

'What about Ned?'

'You know well yourself what happens to Ned. He stays here, and looks after the farm. Fanny can't do it. Nor can we leave her and Mary and Grandfather with no-one able-bodied to defend them.'

'He won't like it, Garret.'

'That's his cross.' Garret opened the door and picked up his hat. 'Let's start.'

'Halt!' Cornelius Sinnott reined in his horse very smartly for a pike was pointing straight at him. 'What have you been telling my brothers?'

Mr Sinnott relaxed. 'Get out of my way,' he said. 'You'll hear soon enough.' He dug his heels into the horse's flanks, only to find the pike resting against his stomach.

'You should be careful,' Ned warned. 'I am needing the practice.'

Mr Sinnott pushed the weapon aside. 'Where did you find it?' he asked.

34

'There's a hundred or more in the wood, and they're sharp grand things.'

'You think you could push one into an English soldier? I doubt it. Stop that!' Ned jabbed the pike against his ribs.

'Tell me what's happening then.'

'The whole strength of the National Directory was arrested yesterday, but not Lord Edward Fitzgerald. We have to rouse the countryside at once!'

Ned ran up the drive towards the house.

'You've dropped the pike! A queer rotten soldier you'd make!'

But Garret and Billy had left. He ran through the house calling for them. Fanny came hurrying downstairs.

'A fine noise you're making,' she scolded. 'What's the matter? They'll not be back here till tomorrow night. And what, may I ask, have you been up to with Ellen?'

He stood quite still, aware of his heartbeat when the name was mentioned.

'Something, I can see,' Fanny went on. 'I've had Mrs Kennedy here complaining that Ellen was hours late coming home last night, and you talking with her in the orchard, she said, sitting very close to her, she said, arm in arm, she said.'

'What's wrong with that?' Ned asked. 'That nosy old woman meddles and gossips too much.' He walked upstairs. 'Are you making tea, Fanny? I'm thirsty.' He went into his room and lay on his bed, looking into the mirror. Was he the most handsome of the brothers? He stared at his face. It was longer, more oval than Garret's or Billy's, and his eyes were greener. He was glad his hair was so dark; Ellen had said she liked it. He enjoyed showing her how strong he was; only the other day he had impressed her by lifting a pile of timber that neither Garret nor Billy could move. He put the mirror down and smiled at his vanity.

35

The baby in the next room started to cry. He put his head round the door, but Mary was already there, rocking the cradle. She raised a finger to her lips, motioning him to be silent. Ned thought her face looked swollen as if she had been weeping. He went downstairs and tried to persuade Fanny to tell him where Garret and Billy had gone.

Mr Sinnott had come with news for Garret, but he was out. Fanny was in the drawing room, sewing; Mary was in the garden with Dermot. Ned poured glasses of beer, one for the draper, one for himself, and offered him the best chair in the kitchen. It was a good moment to ask questions.

'Have they discovered yet who betrayed the Directory?'

'No. But I'm guessing it's Thomas Reynolds.'

'Who's he?'

'A friend of Lord Edward's. He didn't arrive at the meeting, and he's not been seen since. I'm thinking he's surely a government spy.'

'How can a man do that? Betray all his friends for money?'

'It happens often enough. We trust a power of fellows in this business we are not after knowing the characters of.'

'What is the Directory?'

'You should know that. There are four, one for each of the provinces, Ulster, Leinster, Munster, and Connaught. And the National Directory of the United Irishmen above them: they will be forming the government of the republic when we have thrown the English into the sea.'

'And who is Oliver Bond?'

'You ask too many questions! He's a wool merchant, a Leinster delegate to the National Directory, like your cousin William Michael. They were met at ten in the morning in the parlour of his house in Bridge Street. They

were to talk of one thing only, an immediate uprising,
French help or not. I should think they would have voted in
favour, but before they could even begin the place was alive
with the militia. There's a certain humour about it.'

'Why?'

'They can't be charged with any offence. The soldiers
were taking the house to pieces and ripping up floorboards,
and tearing down the chimney brick by brick, may the Lord
rot them! Every man was stripped and searched. There was
not one document, not one single scrap of paper that would
send any man of them before a judge. Now they're sitting
quietly in jail while the government racks its brains trying to
find something to charge them with, for it isn't yet a
criminal offence to visit Mr Bond's house at ten o'clock
in the morning. While we and thousands more decent men
of Ireland, I'm telling you, are sure to be wounded or
killed.'

'You think that's humorous?'

'Not exactly. But it makes me laugh all the same. So do
some other things. May I have another drink?' Ned poured
it, and waited for him to continue. 'God reward your sister;
it's exceedingly good beer. No. The English don't know
how many leaders are still free. They'll surely be wasting a
power of time and men looking for others who are lying
low; the Wexford delegate who was delayed on his journey
is an instance: he saw the soldiers from outside and didn't go
into the house, but ran off into hiding. But you can't help
admiring the spectacle of such an arrest! Twelve members of
an alternative government, in one swift swoop! It's breath-
taking.'

'And probably means the whole plan of things for us all in
ruins.'

'Not at all. They were hard politicians, not military men.'

37

'A wet winter, a dry spring, a bloody summer, and no King.'

'Yes. It's happening.'

Mary came in. Cornelius Sinnott stood up, and reaching for his hat, said, 'I'll be away now to look for Billy and Garret.'

When he had gone, Ned stayed, thinking Mary wanted to talk, but she seemed preoccupied with hunting for something in the pantry. He was just going out of the room when she turned and said, 'A bloody summer, Ireland's fall, no husband, and chaos for us all. That's my prophecy.'

He looked at her a moment, not knowing what to reply, then went out into the yard.

'What right have you to forbid me to do anything? No right at all!'

'Be patient,' said Billy quickly, before Garret could reply.

'I am being patience itself!' his brother thundered, deliberately switching his anger on to Billy. 'Ned, please remember this.' His voice was quieter. 'I'm leaving behind a young wife and a baby son not yet one year old. It's trusting you more than any living man to ask you to look after them. Will you do it, Ned?'

'It's blackmail, Garret. I'd give anything to go with you. I'd always understood that if there was a rising, if the English . . . you know I'm as strong as an ox; I'm a man now, not a boy . . . you'll need me . . . I can use a pike as well as you if not better!'

'I believe you.' Garret crossed the room, and with an unusual surge of warmth embraced his brother. 'You'd endure better than most, that I know, and probably be more violent with a pike. But if all three of us were killed, if the English won, what would happen to that wife and child and

38

sister, alone in this house with just one very old man to protect them? You're old enough to know what victorious soldiers will do. And what could Grandfather do to stop them? There is only you.'

'Blackmail. Half-truth, half-lies. The women can go to our cousins at Cabinteely who are sure to be neutral, being half-English and Protestants. Didn't George marry the sister of an English earl? You just think I'm not old enough, that's all it is!'

'Ned. Please.'

Ned sighed. 'Very well. But on one condition. If the women decide to go to Cabinteely I'll take them there, but once they're in safety I shall do as I like.'

Garret thought for a while. 'It's a bargain then,' he said. 'And we'll drink on it.' He fetched whiskey and glasses from the cupboard.

Billy had not been joking when he told Ned he feared that the sound of every horse might indicate the arrival of soldiers to arrest him. He wondered whether to go into hiding, but Garret convinced him that such a step was over-reacting to the situation, and, besides, what would the peasantry think? The two brothers were looked up to as leaders, men who would help to save honest country folk from the harsh poverty-stricken way of life that was the consequence of English rule. If Billy seemed to be running away, it would make them lose heart. So he did not leave, but his eyes were always alert for any sign of danger; and a horse was kept saddled and ready for him in the stable twenty-four hours a day, just in case.

One morning he was out riding, intending to visit Michael Breen, who lived alone in a cabin some five miles down the Tinahely road. Michael, who had been cowman at

Ballymanus in Grandfather's time, was now old and sick; Billy carried with him some food Fanny had prepared and a pair of stockings knitted by Mary: gifts to the old man from the family.

When he turned a bend in the road he found his way blocked by two horsemen, Protestant neighbours he had occasionally observed in the distance but never once spoken to, both young farmers. The spot was lonely: not a house in sight, and the hillside above shrouded in gloomy woods. He was scared, sensing trouble.

There was a noise behind him, and turning his head he saw three more riders galloping out of the trees. 'That's Billy Byrne!' one of them shouted, which seemed to be a signal for the two who were stationary in the road to move their horses in his direction and urge them on with their whips.

Billy did not wait another second. He flicked his reins, and, vaulting the hedge to his right, he charged down the hillside, desperately hoping the animal's hooves would not find pot-holes or boulders. 'You won't get away that easily!' came a cry from behind him. 'We're going to teach you a lesson! One that you'll surely remember!' He recognized the voice: Matthew Gowan, the son of an old enemy of his father's. The Gowans, neighbouring land-owners and Protestants, had more than once quarrelled with the Byrnes, mainly over fences and boundaries. In the Byrnes' opinion the Gowans were little better than thugs. One of the sons was an officer in the Wicklow Yeomen Cavalry: which was obviously why they were after him now.

His attackers, very slowly, were gaining ground; if they caught him before he reached Ballymanus, a severe beating with horse-whips was certain. 'Come on! Come on!!' he shouted at his horse, but he could expect no more from the beast than she was giving. She jumped gates and ditches with ease, spurred on by sensing Billy's fear; the trouble was she simply hadn't the speed of Gowan's animal.

But luck was with him. When still a good half mile from the edge of the Ballymanus fields, Matthew, well ahead of his friends and only a yard or two behind Billy, stumbled and fell. 'Don't wait for me! Go after him!' Matthew cried when his friends slowed down; and he cursed them frantically when they stopped and helped him instead of continuing the pursuit of Billy. 'Don't think that's the last you've heard of us!' he yelled. 'There's always another time, Billy Byrne!'

Billy arrived home, panting and sweating, covered from head to foot in mud. It was some while before he was able to draw sufficient breath to tell Garret the story.

'You'd best stay on the farm from now on,' Garret said. 'If you must go out, take somebody with you.'

'It won't always be possible.'

'If you are alone . . . then be very careful.' Which was advice, Billy thought, that he hardly needed: the experience had almost terrified him out of his wits.

'And Michael Breen's dinner? And his stockings?'

Garret considered. 'I'll take them myself. And Ned can come as my escort, armed to the teeth if he likes.'

'He'll enjoy that.'

'Yes. I imagine he will!'

So the gifts were delivered. Ned was quite disappointed: there was no sign of Gowan and his henchmen on the journey there or back, indeed no occasion to use his weapons or ride at breakneck speed through the mud.

'Your turn will come,' Garret said, laughing.

Ned had been doing odd jobs round the farm all day, and smelled of it. Mary left the room soon after he came in, which offended him: he thought she probably objected to the aroma. He sprawled in the big chair by the kitchen fire, one leg dangling over its arm. He pushed his bishop across the chess-board and threatened Fanny's knight.

'I took my boots off and left them at the door, didn't I? And my coat. You can't manage a farm without a little piece of dung—'

'Ned! Language.'

'And I had a good wash. Not that I was needing it much; the rain hasn't stopped all day. The only time I was dry was helping to deliver the calf. Check.'

'Why, what else have you been doing?'

'Knocking in fence posts, for the lot of them were blown down in that last gale. Weeding turnips and mucking out the yard. No wonder I smell. Fanny, move that back! Do you want me to have your queen?'

Fanny concentrated on her game. 'Someone has to work,' she said eventually. 'Garret and Billy are out playing silly games of soldiers and where it will all end I don't know. They'll get themselves killed and the house will be confiscated and ourselves with nowhere to lay our heads.'

'The starving people of Ireland will be free and I shall have your queen next move.'

'And God knows we'll not be the better off or happier.'

Ned helped himself to the white queen. 'Isn't it strange,' he said, 'that they called that baby Dermot, and it's such an ugly name! In English it stands for Jeremiah and that's even worse. And in Latin, do you remember the christening? Demetrius. Like that silly fellow in Shakespeare. Yes, I have read some Shakespeare. I'm not all bone in the skull, sister.'

'It's Mary's father's name.'

42

'The eldest son of the eldest son in this family has always been Garret. Father was Garret, and Grandfather before him, and his father before that.'

'The one before that was Hugh. Check. Checkmate! What a hare-brain you are! With being so busy trying to kill me off you didn't look to your own defence! Your king's trapped neatly behind that row of pawns.' Fanny laughed. She very rarely got the better of any of her brothers in games of skill.

Ned grinned and stretched. His feet were almost in the fire; steam rose from his stockings. 'Fetch me my dinner, woman of the house.'

'Fetch it yourself,' she said, then rose and went to the oven. She adored her three brothers, Ned in particular. He was twelve when their mother had died; Fanny's greatest pleasure in life had been feeding, clothing, teaching Little Ned. It never occurred to her that there could be another life than Ballymanus, and cooking and cleaning for her menfolk. She could survive, perhaps, if anything happened to Garret or Billy, but if it was Ned it would kill her. She dreaded the day he would leave home.

'My son will be called Garret.'

Fanny put the plate in front of him and looked at him sharply. 'I didn't know we were in the way to expect such an event!'

'It's a sour tongue you have, sister.' He liked to put on a strong Irish accent at times, the brogue of the country people. 'I've as good a right to beget children as any, though I doubt it's cut out for a father I am at all at all.'

There was a knock on the door: it was Mr Sinnott with a piece of horrifying news. A party of soldiers had been sent from Arklow to arrest a Mr Renehan who lived at Tinahely, not far from Ballymanus. He was suspected, quite rightly, of being deeply involved with the United Irishmen; whether he should have been present at the meeting at Bond's or not Mr Sinnott did not know. He was away from home when the soldiers arrived, and they questioned his wife. She refused to tell them where her husband was, so they made her a pitch-cap.

'A pitch-cap?' Fanny asked. 'What is that?'

'I will tell you,' Mr. Sinnott continued, his voice shaking a little, 'not because I want to be scaring you, but you should be warned. They covered her head with tar, and set light to it. It is not something that would kill you, but it is a torment out of Hell and disfigures you for life. The hair is all burned off the head, which is why these torturers call their victims croppies. This poor woman's screams could be heard for hours.'

'They must be rooted out of this world!' Ned cried.

Ned was woken out of a deep sleep just after dawn by the sound of pistol shots very close to the house. For a moment he thought the rebellion had started, and leaping out of bed he ran to the window. Grandfather was standing in the doorway below him firing at birds. Ned threw the window open just as he fired a second time. The noise was shattering.

'You old fool! Stop it!' Ned shouted, as a starling thudded on to the gravel. 'That gun is so old you will kill yourself!'

Grandfather fired again. 'Another Englishman will be feeling the blood drip from his heart!' he shouted, and, as a pigeon fell out of the sky, he looked up at Ned and grinned. 'I'll destroy every one of them! There'll not be an English soldier left in Ireland!' His eyes were crazy with joy.

He's going mad, Ned thought. 'Will you stop it, Grandfather! You'll wake the whole house!'

There was another ear-splitting explosion, and an alarming quantity of smoke rose from the gun. Billy came out and put his arm round the old man. He could always do things with Grandfather when other people failed.

'Come back to bed,' he said, gently. 'We'll kill the rest of them after breakfast. It's too early in the day for the death of every English soldier in the land.'

Grandfather subsided, and Billy led him indoors. Ned listened to the profound silence the explosions seemed to have produced. Then a stairboard creaked. Birds started to sing again. A swallow darted under the thatch above him. So would the English return, he thought gloomily, whatever we did.

A crunch of feet on the gravel, and there were Billy and Garret in conversation. They were picking up the dead birds and throwing them into the copse.

'There's two hundred more pikes in there,' said Garret. 'I don't know how Thade Keogh has the power.'

'He's a good blacksmith, and so are his brothers, Con and Seán, and their children. And they employ a dozen others who can use any implement in a forge.'

Ned stared at them from the window. Billy certainly had the look of a priest. Father William Byrne, S.J., Archbishop of Armagh, Primate of All Ireland. Pope . . . no, a simple country curate, that was Billy. Priests, some of them on the run, stayed in the house from time to time; Mass had often been said in the drawing room. He watched Billy picking up the dead birds, and something occurred to him that Garret had already noticed: Billy was very ill-equipped for a fight against the English. He could not compromise, and he could not stop being indiscriminately kind.

Ned was climbing up on the moors far above Ballymanus. On the far side of the valley the land curved away into an immense distance until it met a sky full of greyness sweeping majestically in from the Irish Sea. Sheep and cows grazing across there were not much more than black or white dots, and where the valley sides grew steep, great trees and overhanging rocks that had towered above him became innocuous details on the great expanse of things. A stream sang sonorously in the bottom. Above, a raven coughed.

'Ned! Where are you? Wait for me! Ned!!'

He flopped down behind a rock, panting, and listened to Ellen's footsteps. When she was a yard away she shouted again. 'Ned! You're so selfish! Wait for me!'

He stood up as quietly as he could and imprisoned her in his arms. She gave a little shriek, and struggled a little; he was enjoying the moment, then he let her go: an uncaged bird.

'You're small,' he said. 'I could fold myself right round you, and I'm so big, like the wrapping round a parcel.'

'You're an idiot!' After a while she added 'Ned, I think you're becoming more than fond of me.'

He looked away, embarrassed. 'I don't know,' he muttered, and began to hurl stones into the valley. She waited for him to stop.

'Yes,' he said, surprised to hear himself admit the strength of his emotions aloud.

It was unsafe to make such a leap, like rushing headlong into the valley; would he crash down out of control and hurt himself?

She put her arms round his neck and kissed him.

'What does that mean?'

'I love you.'

Pleasure at those words swelled through him; and he kissed her with real feeling. They lay on the grass and were silent for a long while.

'Ned. I have a fearful worry.'

46

'What is it?'

'That you'll go off with Garret and Billy.'

He moved uneasily. 'I promised them I would not. Though God knows I want to.'

'And leave me behind. What happens to me if you're killed?'

'Ellen—don't.' He stuck his pipe in his mouth and chewed the end of it. He had nothing to light the tobacco with.

'Ned. Don't go with them, I beg you!'

'I told them if the women went to Cabinteely then I would surely do as I pleased, and they agreed that I should.'

'Ned—'

'Don't nag at me! You're just like my sister! And spoiling a beautiful day!'

There was a quiver at the corner of her mouth, but he wouldn't relent. Nobody was going to own him, least of all a girl. More blackmail! But she was beautiful and he loved her. Her hair was auburn, soft and long, and she was so tiny, no more than five feet tall—he had to stoop right down to kiss her—and he would go to the wars, and she would be there when he came back.

They stayed a long time in each other's arms and returned home hours late. Ned walked hand in hand with Ellen up to her door.

'Where have you been?' her mother stormed at her. 'Where have you been?' But she became quite silent when she saw Ned towering up in front of her.

That evening he sat in front of the kitchen fire, unusually silent. He lost three more games of chess with Grandfather, and smoked so many pipes of tobacco that Fanny commented that the fog in Dublin City could be no worse, and what in Heaven was ailing him now?

Cornelius Sinnott came early next day. There was a long whispered conversation with Garret and Billy in the parlour. Ned, in and out of the house with buckets of milk, guessed this meant they would be leaving soon. But they seemed in no hurry. Other callers came and went, some looking cheerful, some depressed, some obviously bringing exciting news. Late in the afternoon, Ned, in the field furthest from the house, looking for pigeons to shoot, thought he heard the sound of distant gun-fire, far off towards the sea. But it could have been thunder; it was grey and uneasy in that direction, though the sun shone on Ballymanus. Once Billy rode out at furious speed on a white horse; his hat and cloak were white and Ned thought he looked like a saint in battle. He returned half an hour later on a different horse, a piebald. Towards evening groups of armed men appeared on the drive. They stood there in twos and threes, chatting, smoking, comparing weapons. Garret went out and walked from group to group, shaking hands, explaining, exhorting. More men arrived, armed with pikes; eventually there must have been about a hundred. Ned recognized most of them, farm labourers, servants, shop-keepers, blacksmiths of the neighbourhood. At about six o'clock they all left, mostly on foot, but some on horseback, a ragged procession, making for Shillelagh it looked like. Mr Sinnott, who seemed to occupy some position of authority like a sergeant, went with them. He was driving a covered wagon, laden with provisions. Two other horse-drawn carts, Thade and Seán Keogh at the reins, followed him. These carts were loaded with murderous-looking pikes, straight from the forge, new and gleaming in the thin evening sunlight.

Still Garret and Billy did not go. The family ate pigeon pie for dinner, and exchanged details of the day's news: the arrest of the ringleaders at Bond's had precipitated a spontaneous uprising in County Kildare.

Garret was tense and nervous. 'Scarcely a single Catholic able to bear arms has failed to answer the call!' he said.

'And most of the poorer Protestants too,' Billy added.

'With what success?' Grandfather asked.

The two brothers looked at each other and laughed. 'Success? I should say there has been a *rout!*' Billy said. 'Except for the towns, the whole of Kildare is in our hands.'

Grandfather was silent, absorbing this. Eventually he stood up and said 'Why . . . I do begin to believe the whole enterprise is going to work! I'd never really thought it was possible!'

Billy laughed again. 'O ye of little faith!'

'Ned, go to the cellar and bring up two bottles of the best wine. This calls for a celebration. At last! At . . . last!!'

Ned did as he was told, and when the wine was uncorked he proposed a toast. 'To the green bough of liberty!'

'To Ireland,' said Garret.

'To us,' Mary said. 'To our safety. May no harm come to any one of us.'

'What has been happening here in Wicklow?' Grandfather asked.

'Things are quiet,' Garret told him. 'The mountains make speed impossible; there has been no general rising of the people as in Kildare or Queen's County or Wexford. We have no citizens' army as such.'

'We should have,' Grandfather said.

'The English will certainly push south from Dublin to meet us in Wexford; reports have come through of heavy fighting there, a vast army of United men besieging Enniscorthy. If Enniscorthy falls then they are to turn north into Wicklow, so we shall see some action. Our task is to halt the English advance through the mountains, at Rathdrum or Baltinglass. That's why our friends and neighbours are marching now to the general meeting point.'

'Where's that?'

'Shillelagh.'

'I can wield a pike as well as any man. Every bird I aimed at the other morning I shot and killed! I've a good mind to go with you.'

'No, Grandfather,' Billy said. 'It's out of the question.'

'Why?'

'Ned, if English soldiers come here while we are away, make sure our valuables are locked in the cellar,' Garret said.

'I will,' Ned answered.

'Why do you take no notice of me?' Grandfather shouted. A little wine always made him belligerent.

'They won't,' Mary said. 'Nor of me.' She heaped reproaches on everyone; it was all somehow proof that the Byrnes, Garret in particular, had never loved her. She went to her room in tears, and Garret, after a few more words with Billy, followed her.

Fanny said nothing.

Ned woke before dawn from a dream in which he and Ellen were both riding the same horse, wildly out of control, across a battlefield. There were shots, and cries of the dying.

He sat upright in bed, and listened to the horses' hooves crunching the gravel, then a more blurred noise as they reached the road. They were travelling in a southerly direction. Ned listened until he could hear only the silence, then went to sleep again. Garret and Billy had gone.

50

CHAPTER THREE

ROUNDWOOD

News of brutal cruelties came daily to the Ballymanus household. Parties of English soldiers installed themselves in villages that were thought to be strongly on the insurgents' side, demanding 'free quarters', food, lodging and forage for their horses. These demands were readily met after a few people had been decorated with pitch-caps. Women were raped; thatched roofs set on fire, sometimes for the fun of it rather than because a rebel was thought to be hiding there; men and women were shot for being slow in giving information, or their children were killed or muti-lated in front of their eyes; old men were murdered, asleep in their beds; 'triangles' were set up in the centres of villages— these were three-sided wooden frames—and men tied to them and given two or three hundred lashes in order to coax out information or to punish some supposed petty misdemean-our. Many were beaten till their bones showed through the torn flesh; many died before the flogging ceased. This was the news from the north, from Meath and County Dublin. From Wexford there was a different story. Enniscorthy had fallen to the rebels, though instead of marching north as expected, they were streaming towards Wexford City. New Ross was about to fall; the garrison was on the point of capitulation. But reports of the rebels' behaviour suggested that some of their excesses were as bad as the enemy's.

Ned knew the women were frightened. The slightest incident would persuade them it would be safer to move to Cabinteely. His own resolution, to go and join his brothers as soon as Fanny and Mary were settled there, hardened with each piece of new information. He practised with a pistol and a musket, incessantly, on the unfortunate bird population of Ballymanus, and taught himself how to handle a pike. He began to think seriously about all the implications of killing a man and tried to discuss it with Ellen. Their relationship was in a high state of tension, moving from delight as they began to learn how much they loved each other, to tears and sullenness whenever Ned's plans for the future were mentioned. He slept badly, waking up with a jolt from frightening dreams. Even the few comforting messages that came from Garret and Billy, telling him where they were and what successes they had had against the enemy, so many English dead, so few of their own side killed, failed to calm him.

One fine morning in late May English troops arrived at Ballymanus, and the ensuing events destroyed this tension. It was action he had been waiting for, and when it came at last he was happier.

Fanny, looking out of an upper window, noticed them first. A party of soldiers was wheeling a cannon through a field on the far side of the road that passed the gates of Ballymanus. For a moment they were lost to view behind some trees, but the field sloped steeply uphill, and they soon emerged. The cannon was slowly pivoted round so that it was pointing, it seemed to Fanny, straight at her. She ran out of the room and down the stairs, shrieking for Ned, who came running to the back of the house, a pitchfork in his hand. Grandfather opened the door of his room in mild surprise, and Mary looked up from feeding Dermot, her eyes full of fear.

'They are going to blast the house to pieces!' Fanny screamed. 'For God's sake run outside!' And she dashed to the front door, followed by Ned, who was still holding the pitchfork; but before they reached it it was kicked open. Several armed men stood there.

A lieutenant in a red coat, who appeared to be the leader, demanded: 'Where is Garret Byrne?'

'He is not at home,' replied Fanny. 'He has been away now for several weeks.'

'With brother Billy, no doubt?'

'Yes, sir.'

'They are United Irishmen, are they not?'

'Yes, sir,' said Fanny, 'but we are not.'

'Fanny!' exclaimed Ned, furious at her treachery.

'Search the house! We'll soon find out the truth!' About twenty men, some in soldiers' uniforms, rushed into the hall. Fanny ran upstairs, followed by Ned, who had dropped his pitchfork, realizing it would be mistaken for a weapon. There was a deafening explosion as they reached the corner of the stairs which momentarily checked not only their own progress, but the soldiers' as well. On the landing was Grandfather, firing a musket at one of the invaders, a shot which missed and lodged in the floor.

'Old fool, do you want to destroy us all?' Ned shouted, and, seizing the gun, he pulled it from the old man's hands, and threw it over the balustrade to one of the soldiers, who caught it.

This action ensured that they would, for the time being, remain unharmed, and the soldiers seemed more interested anyway in searching the rooms, which they did with a great

55

deal of shouting and swearing when they found no sign of the missing brothers.Crockery crashed to the floor in the kitchen, and Mary rushed out holding Dermot who was screaming, and joined the others on the stairs. From the upper rooms came the sound of tearing linen, pictures being ripped from walls, windows smashing. A man came casually out of the kitchen, drinking wine from a bottle, and pushed over the grandfather clock in the hall. It fell on its face, glass splintering, its insides protesting in a jangling discord. Fanny burst into tears, and Ned shouted curses.

The lieutenant came to the foot of the stairs. He seemed to be enjoying himself immensely. Ned wished he had an evil face, but it was quite ordinary. He was a small man, and spoke in a dialect Ned could not identify.

'Where are your brothers?'

'We don't know.'

'Have you had letters from them? Any other kind of message?'

'No.'

'We'll see if you change your mind, lad. A flogging may help you concentrate.'

Ned ran across the landing, but four men coming out of a bedroom seized him and dragged him, kicking, biting and scratching, down the stairs, and out through the front door. A few yards from the house was a large wooden frame—the dreaded triangles.

'Tie him to that,' someone shouted. 'Thrash him till he speaks.'

Ned's shirt was torn from his back, and his hands and feet bound tightly to the instrument of punishment. It had just started to rain, and the water felt like needle pricks on his warm bare arms and shoulders.

'Read these,' cried Fanny, running out of the house.

'Here are their letters! I couldn't find them at first, for the kitchen is ransacked. These will tell you!'

'Fanny!' shouted Ned. 'Don't show them! Tear them up!'

'And be seeing you cut to ribbons!'

'I can stand a flogging. I shan't betray my brothers to this scum!'

'Lash him for that!' cried one of the men.

'Yes,' said the lieutenant. 'Two strokes. After all he's only a child, isn't he? Let him see if he wants more after that.'

'And keep your tongue still!' cried Fanny.

The cat of nine tails left its giant red imprints on Ned's shoulders. The rain slowly washed the blood down his back into his breeches. He shivered, although the day was sultry, and he thought he was going to collapse: the pain was excruciating. But inwardly he felt calm. There would be no difficulty now in killing men, either with bullets or a pike.

The lieutenant scanned the letters. 'They seem in order, Miss Byrne,' he said, his voice suddenly becoming polite. 'All we want is a little co-operation. Your brother, by the way, could be dangerous, so we'll leave him out in the rain for a while.' He shouted to his men, 'Call off the search! Come outside!' Turning to Fanny, he said, 'This is too pleasant a place. I think we should make it more difficult for you.'

'Then can we leave, sir?' Fanny begged.

'Leave? Oh yes, no doubt you will want to!' He laughed.

Some of the men came out of the house, carrying pieces of blazing wood taken from the kitchen fire, and burning rags. They threw these up on to the thatch. In spite of the rain, the roof was on fire from end to end within minutes. The rest of the soldiers soon hurried out of the house and stood watching it burn. The last person to come out was Grandfather, who was carrying his box full of deeds, wills and letters.

57

The lieutenant watched for a moment, then he ordered his men to leave. Ned was cut from the triangles, but his hands and feet were re-bound in case he should do any mischief. He was left lying face downwards in the mud. The triangles were placed on the cart, and the whole party of soldiers moved off in twos and threes, a bedraggled procession, oddly reminiscent of the party of rebels who had left on that fine evening some weeks before.

Mary knelt on the grass, cowering over Dermot, who was still shrieking with terror. She was too shocked to speak or move. Grandfather stood, dazed, watching the flames crackle and the column of black smoke rise upwards. Smoke was now coming from the windows on the second storey. Black ash spiralled in the air. Fanny rushed indoors and emerged with a knife to free Ned. She helped him into the house and dressed his wounds in the kitchen; there seemed no danger of fire as yet on the ground floor, though the smoke in the air made them cough.

Ned lay face down on the table while Fanny washed the great cuts left by the whip. He gritted his teeth against the pain, and swore every foul word he could think of. When she had finished he stood up and, seizing a glass vase, hurled it with all his strength at the wall. It smashed to tiny pieces.

'That's what I'll do to them! Let them wait, that's all! *Bastards!*'

'We're going to Cabinteely, Ned.'

'Yes . . . yes . . . we should,' he said. 'We have no choice.'

'You were lucky,' said Fanny. 'I don't understand you. It was right, oh yes it was, snatching the gun from Grandfather. But those lashes were your own fault, and you were lucky, very lucky, it wasn't two hundred stripes on your back!'

'You betrayed Garret and Billy. I shan't forgive you!'

'I did not. I showed him the very first letter we had, and Garret and Billy will be miles away from there by now.'

'Pandering to barbarians—'

'Do you want us all to be shot or flogged? You should be a man, Ned! Grow up!'

He said, grimly, 'I've grown up all right. My poor back is a burning fiery furnace!' He moved his arms and shoulders very gingerly.

'It won't be painful for too long after the sting dies out of it. Go and find a clean shirt.'

Mary and Grandfather came in, very wet. The rain had increased and the fire was now only smouldering.

'We'll be leaving for Cabinteely,' said Fanny. 'There's one cart outside that Garret left, and a horse. As soon as the rain eases. I'll go now and pack.'

'And who will stay to look after the house?' Grandfather asked.

'Mrs Kennedy, perhaps.'

'She will not. Ellen and she will go with you.'

'The house is a ruin, anyway.'

'Nonsense!'

They went outside to look. The fire, thanks to the downpour, was nearly out, but the rain was filled with ash and pieces of straw, like black snow. The roof was totally destroyed, charred rafters protruding through the remnants of the thatch. The top storey was uninhabitable; some of the rooms were open to the sky as the ceilings had burned. All the attic windows had broken, either from the heat, or because the soldiers had smashed them. The whitewashed walls above were smeared with black. But the first floor and the ground floor were undamaged, at least from the fire. The women began to weep again.

'I shall stay here,' said Grandfather.

'You will not,' said Fanny, her tears stopping at once.

'I will! I was born here and nobody is going to make me move! Not you, nor a crowd of English shoneens.'

'You will die of pneumonia! If it rains for any length it will go straight through to your bedroom.'

'Don't let us argue out in the wet,' said Mary.

They returned to the kitchen and argued for a long time. Fanny gave way at last, for the old man would not budge. He was full of plans for repairs to the roof; at daylight he was going to send for his neighbours. Luke O'Toole and John Nolan owed the farm two days' work each; Darby Whelan, the carpenter, would come with wood. There was spare reed in the barns, or tiles to be had at Patterson's; and Jude Quinlan, the thatcher, was still around, for he had refused to go off with the rebels. Ned and Mary went to pack, while Fanny changed her mind and began to shout at Grandfather again. Eventually she was defeated, and went to find clothes and sheets and other necessities no-one else would have thought of.

When they were ready, Grandfather gave Fanny a purse containing forty pounds.

'I had no idea there was such money in the house,' she said, amazed, and rather shocked.

'And this box,' the old man went on, 'contains all your mother's and your grandmother's jewellery, except for a ring which Garret has, and the cross Billy wears round his neck. Take them; what are you gaping at? And this'—he handed her several very old sheets of parchment—'is the Byrne family tree.'

'What in the world should I want with that?'

'It may turn out to be more valuable than all those precious stones. It proves our relationship to the Byrnes of Cabinteely.'

60

'We know that they're cousins, you old fool. Distant cousins.'

'They'll be neutral. Some of them are Protestants, and have great influence; you may need their help. If the United Irishmen are beaten, and Garret and Billy taken, these pieces of paper may save their lives.'

'Save their lives? You mean they might be . . . hanged?'

'Yes.'

'But—'

'Stop contradicting,' Ned put in. 'What did you expect? If they were taken prisoner, they'd be for the hangman. You know that, Fanny. Grandfather is quite right.' He took the papers and placed them in the jewel box.

A little time later they left, Fanny and Mary with baby Dermot, now asleep, huddled between the luggage on the open cart, trying, with rugs and blankets, to keep out the streaming rain. Ned, protected only by a huge old cape and a hat, was at the front, acting as coachman.

They stopped at Mrs Kennedy's. Ellen was at the door; Ned jumped down from the cart and kissed her, unworried by the presence of the others.

'We saw the roof burning, and the soldiers leaving—'

He winced. 'Don't touch my back!'

'Ned, we know. Luke O'Toole saw you, and told us on his way home. Ned, how could they—'

'We think you should both come with us to Cabinteely.'

Mrs Kennedy appeared in the doorway. 'I guessed you would soon be going, so I've packed all our things and we're ready. Luke will look after Ballymanus and this cottage, though God knows I don't expect to see them standing if I return. You can help Ned with this trunk, Ellen.'

Mrs Kennedy took her place on the cart, wedged between Mary's luggage and her own. Ellen crept up against Ned at

61

the front, underneath the big cape. They drove down the road towards Aughrim, in silence.

'I must tell you this,' Ned said at last. 'I'm going from Cabinteely to find my brothers. There's nothing you can say can shake me from it, so don't try. But I shall be back; I know it in my bones that nothing will happen to me. There . . . there's something else, too.'

'What is it?'

'I don't know how I should say it, but when . . . when I come back I . . . I want us to marry, Ellen.'

She did not reply. 'We are only eighteen,' she said after a while. 'Our families will not think it right.'

'Time is short now, though I know I shall be returning. I'll see much, these next weeks or months. Ellen, I can't go without knowing. It will make me . . . survive.'

'Of course I will.'

They drew closer together. Ned wanted to leap and dance on the cart for joy, but he had to hold the reins of the horse steady.

'Ellen. That ring you can feel now on my little finger, take it. It's yours. It's from the family jewel box. I can't use my right hand, or the horse will take us into the hedge.'

It was an old signet ring, with a ruby, that had been Ned's mother's; it fitted the second finger on Ellen's left hand.

'We will have it altered,' he said, 'so it fits the third finger.'

Ellen was too overcome to reply, and they continued in comfortable silence, unaware of the drenching rain. Behind them the three women went over the events of the day. Dermot slept.

They passed very few people, nor was there sign of rebels or soldiers. Once, in the deepening gloom, they passed a group of men slouching by a gate, and Ned felt behind him for the loaded guns and pistols, dry under a blanket. But they did no more than bid the people on the cart good evening, and wished them soon in the dry. Ned sighed.

'What are you thinking?' Ellen asked.

'All our smashed things. Chairs and beds on the top floor charred and burnt. In my bedroom they ripped open the mattress; the floor's all covered in feathers. And Billy's crucifix. It looked as if it had been hit with a hammer; the arms and feet still sticking there and the head and body in bits. And, God help me, but my back is so stiff! The weals on my shoulders feel like fire. Bastards!' He spat into the road.

Ned drove on late into the dark; before they reached Aughrim Mrs Kennedy, Fanny and Mary were asleep, and Ellen was nodding and swaying against him. Ned wondered what sort of reception would greet them in Aughrim; it was not a garrison town but there was no way of knowing whether it was in loyalist or rebel hands, or whether it had remained untouched by the rising. It was about ten o'clock when they arrived at the outskirts, and there was no-one to be seen. Right through the streets to the centre and beyond it was the same; not a light, not a voice, not a shadow of a man moving anywhere. It was completely deserted. Ned wondered much at this, and could think of no explanation; there was no destruction visible, no burnt houses, no sign of a fight. The people seemed to have vanished. But as they went down the valley, he noticed movements and sounds in the fields and odd lights moving, and he heard strange muffled voices. This was very frightening, and he urged the horse on as rapidly as it was able. He was nodding asleep himself, and longed for something soft to rest on to ease his smarting back, but he forced himself on, thinking it would be safer to travel at night. Before Rathdrum he left the main road to avoid the town, feeling it might be hostile or eery as Aughrim; there was a choice of roads, through the mountain passes, or down to Wicklow and the coast. He took the mountain road, remembering there were troops stationed at Wicklow and Bray, but stopped after a mile he was so stiff with weariness. Half-asleep on his feet, he remembered to jump from the cart and turn the horse loose, then clambered into the luggage with the sleeping Ellen in his arms, but was lost to consciousness before he could appreciate this enormous privilege.

Next day dawned fine and warm, and was the start of a heatwave that was to last the summer through. Ned woke first, and without waking the others harnessed the horse and drove on. They stopped to eat by an old churchyard at Glendalough. Fanny had put a quantity of food on the cart, and she made a makeshift breakfast. The dry weather and sunshine and the beauty of the scenery seemed to cheer them a little after the tragedy of the day before. When they had eaten they looked at the gravestones, and peeped inside the church, almost as if they were a group of people on holiday.

Ellen's mother had a fancy for graveyards. 'There's a power of Kennedys underneath here,' she said, and led Fanny on a tour of the tombstones. There were indeed many Kennedy inscriptions, but, try as she might, she could not find herself related to any of them.

Mary seemed happy playing with Dermot, and he, too, appeared to have forgotten in the morning sun his fright of the day before. Ned and Ellen stood in the church porch, arms round each other.

'What are you holding, Ellen? You've been clutching to yourself some queer thing since we left the cart.'

She looked shy a moment, then said, 'Bend down. And unbutton your shirt.'

64

He did as he was told, and she placed round his neck a chain from which hung a cross.

'It was my father's,' she said.

'It's the twin of Billy's!'

'They both belonged to our great-grandfather.'

He drew her to him, but said nothing. Her face was against his chest.

'Your skin is warm and smells of yourself. You are a handsome boy, Ned.'

'My back is not.'

She untwined his arms and, pulling his shirt very carefully off his shoulders, looked at the scars. 'My poor Ned!' She put her cheek against the marks.

Mrs Kennedy and Fanny came into view.

'Ellen, why is Ned wearing that cross?'

'I gave it to him.'

Mrs Kennedy turned away with an exclamation of annoyance.

'Cousin Bridget.' Ned went up to her. 'When this war has been won, Ellen and I will be married.'

'What childish thing is this? You're only a boy!'

'Little Ned, this is nonsense,' said Fanny, feebly. Her adored Ned at eighteen, talking about marriage: it didn't make sense, this little brother she had brought up.

'Fanny, we're not twenty-one and therefore we need your consent, or Garret's or Billy's. And I will have it.'

They drove on through the mountains. There were still no signs of rebellion, no troops marching towards them from Dublin; Ned wondered if they existed only in people's imagination. They passed lonely cabins and small clusters of houses: passers-by stared at them more than would be usual; some ran away at the sight of the horse and laden cart. A few greeted them with the country welcome, 'God bless you'; none offered violence. The region, being very mountainous, was sparsely populated. The summits, when the road was high, stretched back for miles, green with unfolding fern and the new season's grass. They saw more sheep than people, and crows and hawks idle in the blue sky, and the most common sounds were waterfalls. When the road descended, the huge rocks, wet from springs above, rose threateningly over them, and twisted birch trees hung from the hillsides' crevices and faults. These were the Wicklow Mountains, famous in autumn for their purple heather, almost the highest peaks in Ireland, the ancient territories of the Clan O'Byrne, the Lords of Ranelagh.

At Roundwood there was plenty that was unusual. A green flag with a golden harp emblazoned on it flew from the roof of the toll-house. There was considerable activity in the village but before they could reach it, a man stepped out in front of the horse. Ned drew in the reins. The man was a strange sight, dressed in an ill-fitting bright green uniform with silver epaulettes.

'What have you in your hand, citizen?' he asked.

Ned smiled. 'A green bough.'

'Where did it first grow?'

'In America.'

'Where did it bud?'

'In France.'

'Where are you going to plant it?'

'In the crown of Great Britain.'

'Cead míle fáilte. This place is republican; it is at liberty. You may pass. Erin go bragh, citizen.'

'I have not the Irish,' said Ned, smiling at the man's eccentric behaviour, 'but I understand you well enough.'

They drove on and stopped in the market square. The

66

women went in search of food; Ned gave oats to the horse and led it to the water trough. Then he went to an ale-house for beer, a pipe to smoke, and news.

True facts about the rebellion were hard to come by. Everyone had tales that suggested a total breakdown of law and order on both sides. There were plenty of frightening stories, but whether the rising was a success or not nobody knew. The towns of County Kildare, Ned learned, were all now in rebel hands except for Naas where hundreds of pikemen had been killed, and Athy, where the insurgents had been cut to pieces. Great victories had been won in County Wexford, at Oulart for instance, and a few hours ago news had come that the government forces had lost Gorey; almost every Protestant in the town had been massacred, and a vast pillar of smoke covered it, visible fifteen miles off. A huge rebel force was about to attack New Ross. Few troops had left Dublin as the authorities feared the capital itself would be besieged. Ned was relieved to hear this; the journey to Cabinteely would be quiet, and he ordered a second pint of ale.

Roundwood had been attacked by a loyalist gang of thugs called the Black Mob whose leader was Hunter Gowan. Ned shivered when he heard the name.

'My father once had a fight with him,' he explained, 'and thrashed him soundly. My brother Billy was nearly horse-whipped by his son, a few weeks back.'

'Who is it, your father?' asked the landlord.

'Garret Byrne of Ballymanus. He died many years ago.'

'Gowan will surely want his revenge. If your father is dead, he may well try for it on you.'

'Perhaps he has done so.' And Ned told him of the previous day's visit the soldiers had paid to Ballymanus.

'It doesn't sound like Gowan', said a man playing dice on

the counter. 'But I would be thinking he put the militia up to it.'

The Black Mob had smashed a lot of windows in Roundwood one evening the previous week and set fire to a number of thatched roofs. At first it had seemed totally pointless, but then they sought out the village blacksmiths and flogged them; they wanted to know the names of those who had placed orders for pikes. Some poor fellows had their heads set alight with pitch-caps, and one had been stabbed to death. The following day Roundwood took the law into its own hands. All the local Protestants were rounded up and locked inside their church, where, Ned was assured, they were being treated very humanely. Armed men guarded all the entries into the village, day and night, in force; Ned thought with amusement of the one unarmed eccentric who had stopped him. He lit a second pipe, and puffed away, listening. These good people had marvels to tell, and here was a sympathetic stranger. The organization of things had been taken over by a committee of citizens, mostly shopkeepers, under the leadership of a grocer. They had the blacksmiths' forges working twenty-four hours a day turning out pikes, and had ordered the tailors to make green uniforms. A Tree of Liberty had been erected in the square, and there was music and dancing every evening.

'Very foreign and French, some of their notions,' growled an old labourer in the chimney corner.

But the conversation kept reverting to brutalities. A wave of panic was beginning to infect the peasantry of Wicklow. The reason why Aughrim was deserted, the landlord explained to Ned, was the people were so terrified of being murdered at night by Orangemen they went out to sleep in the fields. It was happening all over the county, and in

Wexford too. Men had died of heart failure, through nothing but fear. A whole village near Bray had been deliberately poisoned by a loyalist baker who had put arsenic in his loaves.

Ned scoffed at this, and several men agreed. 'You surely cannot believe all that you hear,' they said.

But other stories perhaps had more basis; Hunter Gowan marching into Gorey with the head of one of his victims on the end of his sword; a man hanged from a lamp-post for no offence other than possessing a Catholic prayer-book; rebel sympathizers on their knees, praying for the King and cursing all United Irishmen, in order to avoid a flogging or a pitch-cap: and on the other side, the news of the rebels' victory at Oulart spreading panic among the loyalists; the road north from Gorey choked with escaping townsfolk, women on foot with children on their backs stumbling in the dust; madmen let loose from the Bedlam shrieking in the streets, corpses rotting in the alleys, dogs howling with hunger or feeding on the dead bodies.

Ned had heard enough. He returned the pipe to the landlord, and thanked the company for the news, and in return they wished him a safe journey.

'Arrive before nightfall,' were the landlord's last words. 'The garrison at Bray are wild after dark.'

The yard behind the inn had been turned into a fair-ground; it was the focal point of the village's holiday mood. There were booths selling cheap trinkets, ribbons, buttons and beads; food stalls manned by country folk selling vegetables; an old creaking merry-go-round; coconut shies. There was a large crowd of people, mostly of the poorer class, wandering about aimlessly, but they seemed to have little money to spend. There were many who looked as if they would normally be working, but who had taken the village's 'liberation' as a signal for a holiday. Several drunk men lay on the cobbles. The large number of country people Ned thought might be due to recent events; it was safer to be in Roundwood both day and night than in an isolated cabin out on the moors. A wrestler offered to fight all comers; Ned thought he would probably be his match, but his back was too sore. Instead he threw a coin down at the weight-lifter's stall, and won a few small prizes for raising above his head the largest lump of pig-iron in the booth.

In this atmosphere, the tales of cruelty and murder seemed dubious, products of feverish imagination or hysteria. The rebellion was remote, almost improbable, and he wondered for a moment if it was all a great trick on the part of one or the other side to cower the populace. He had seen no fighting and heard no guns, except for the one incident yesterday at Ballymanus. Perhaps that was just Hunter Gowan's revenge on the Byrnes. Perhaps life would return to normal as suddenly and inexplicably as it had been disrupted; Billy and Garret would come home, the roof be repaired, and the farm go about its usual quiet business. He thought with wry amusement that he might be disappointed if this happened too quickly.

So, affected by the general feeling of well-being, the family continued northwards on the Dublin road.

They stopped to rest by a stream just south of Enniskerry. Dermot was lying naked on a rug, gurgling at a buttercup; Mary washed his soiled clothes in the stream. The others lay on the grass, enjoying the hot afternoon sunshine. Ned was nearly asleep. Ellen stroked his face till he woke and closed his mouth on her fingers.

'Ned! Mary! Look at Dermot *now*!'

The baby was sitting up, the first time he had ever done

70

so. The women exclaimed with delight, and Dermot fell flat on his back.

'Why Ellen,' said Mrs. Kennedy, 'I do believe you were much younger when you first sat upright.'

'He's a clever boy,' said Mary. 'He takes after his father.' She was able to refer to Garret for the first time for weeks without looking as if she might cry.

'Ned was very backward,' Fanny murmured.

'I was not.'

'He's a sweet thing,' said Ellen. 'Do let me hold him.' She picked up the baby and cuddled him.

'He loves you.' Mary flashed a rare smile. 'Just look at the laughter in him.'

'Mind he doesn't wet your dress,' Ned said.

'Why are you always so common?' Fanny asked.

'Wouldn't you like us to have one like this?' Ellen whispered to Ned. 'Isn't he a love? I could dote on him,' and she tickled Dermot, who wriggled and laughed.

Ned was silent. To be a father, the father of Ellen's child, in when—perhaps a year, two years?—was an idea that had never seriously entered his head. His thoughts and feelings about Ellen concerned only the two of them, at breakfast, or in bed at night, or she cooking his dinner, living all the time with just her. He was not sure that he liked babies. They were part of the more inscrutable side of the female world.

'Uncle Ned, hold him.' Ned took the baby clumsily, and at once all the women were telling him what to do, four different sets of instructions on how to hold the baby's head, not to crush him, not to drop him: it had been the same every time he had come near Dermot since the day a few months back when the child was born.

Dermot started to cry. Ned thought again how enormous

71

a baby's head was, compared with the tiny size of the rest of him.

Mary took him.

'His uncle will surely have to learn,' Ellen said, and slipped her hand in his. Ned wanted to push it away, but did not. He wondered for the first time whether the idea of marrying Ellen was not quite mad. Eighteen. There was so much to do that was better than spawning babies. Then he remembered her putting the cross round his neck yesterday, and the touch of her fingers down his skin; and the warmth flowed back in him.

'Enjoying ourselves, are we?' The voice was loud, the accent aristocratic and English. They looked up: an officer, in resplendent new red coat, was standing above them on the road, and a party of twelve armed soldiers in line behind him.

'We are doing no harm at all, sir,' said Mrs Kennedy, as they scrambled to their feet, and Ned felt sick again at the way his family had to be polite and sycophantic to these foreigners, these invaders.

'We shall see,' said the officer. 'While you've been busy down by the water's edge, you failed to see us arrive. We search your cart without you noticing us; we find a quantity of arms, various items of luggage, and a box full of valuable-looking jewellery. Very careless of you, very negligent. Now, what are we to think? Are you thieves? That would account for the jewels. Are you rebels? That would account for the arms.'

'We are neither,' said Ned hotly. 'How can you—'

'Be silent, Ned!' said Fanny, and Ellen kicked him hard on the ankle.

'Perhaps you are spies. I can have you flogged, I hope you realize that. We can march you, young man, to Bray and a

72

few hundred lashes can have most of the flesh off your back.'
He tapped the side of his boot with a cane, rather enjoying
his suggestion.

Ned could not contain himself. 'How should you—'

'Our name is Byrne, sir,' cried Fanny. 'We are loyalists,
and travelling to our cousins, the Byrnes of Cabinteely. The
United men have terrorised our district, sir, and we are
going to our cousins for protection.'

'Byrne of Cabinteely.' The officer's tone changed at once.
He turned to his men. 'All right, you can fall out. Go and
sit on the other side of the road. Byrne of Cabinteely, eh?
That is a big name indeed. Can you prove it?'

'Oh yes, sir. There is a document in one of the boxes, our
pedigree.'

'I have thrown it away, Fanny,' said Ned, quickly. 'I
have, and I'm sorry. I thought it an old scrap of paper of no
use at all.'

'The saints forbid!' Fanny looked appalled, and the other
women turned to him accusingly.

'Are you not Byrnes of Ballymanus?' the officer asked.
'There are two notorious rebels named Byrne from
there.'

Ned was sure the expressions on their faces would give
them away; even Fanny was at a loss for a moment. But
Mary came to the rescue, saying, in a low voice, 'We know
them not, sir. We are from Tinahely.'

The officer thought for a moment. 'If what you say is
true, I should be laughed at if I arrested you. But I'm
suspicious. You had best proceed, but we shall follow you,
not far behind, right up to the doors of Mr Byrne's house. If
you attempt to go anywhere else I shall personally see you
flogged, boy, on the quayside at Bray, until you speak the
truth. And if I don't like the truth you'll be lashed till you're

73

pulp.' He turned and ordered his men to fall in. 'Did you come from Roundwood?' he asked, much more affable.

'Yes sir.'

'You would not know it now. My soldiers have certainly brought a little sense into the people's heads there. The whole village is ablaze from end to end. Rebellion, you see, does not pay.'

Mary led the way back to the cart and they continued their journey in sombre mood. The soldiers followed them, about thirty yards behind, for mile after mile.

'What he was saying about Roundwood,' said Ned, 'is lies. Twelve men against the whole population! I can't believe it. It was said just to frighten us. So be more cheerful, sister.'

'I'm sure you're right,' said Fanny. 'It wasn't that I am sad about. How could you, Ned, throw away that precious old document, how could you?'

Ned laughed. 'It's in the box, or what place you put it. I swear I never touched it.' He laughed again, so much that he almost fell off the cart.

'Ned, I shall never understand you. Why should you tell them you'd thrown it away when we needed to prove the Cabinteely family our cousins?'

'And if you had I should now be marching to Bray for a flogging that would certainly kill me, and you would be on your back in the grass with those twelve louts taking their pleasure.'

'Don't talk like that!'

He grinned. 'Oh, Fanny, my dear little sister! You think you should be the only one clever enough to outwit the enemy, but your poor thick Ned is just as bright.'

'How is it?'

'If he'd seen that document he'd know we were the

74

Byrnes of Ballymanus, wouldn't he? And hasn't it Garret's name, and Billy's name, as well as ours? Oh yes, it would prove our relationship all right!'

Fanny clapped her hands to her mouth at the horror of it. She, Frances Byrne, through sheer stupidity, had nearly destroyed her loved ones!

Ned laughed again. 'Look under the box, Fanny. I have presents there, a rattle for Dermot, and a bangle for each of you from Roundwood fair, and all for lifting up a great lump of pig-iron right over my head.'

'Ned, I'm so sorry! What would we have done without you?'

'My four women and just little Ned to protect them! I'm beginning to enjoy my new role!'

'You'll be coming to a bad end,' said Ellen. 'You're far too conceited.'

He gave her a long kiss.

CHAPTER FOUR

HACKETSTOWN

Robert Byrne Esquire of Cabinteely was the head of the family, senior descendant of the senior branch of the O'Byrnes, the Lords of Ranelagh, who had ruled County Wicklow before the English were even heard of. His father had married Clare Nugent, an English aristocrat, whose brother was Earl Nugent, Lord of the Treasury to King George II. In the present troubles this meant that he was safer than most in Ireland, belonging, as he did, to the English establishment on the one side, and descended on the other from one of the greatest of Irish septs, with an honourable record of resistance to all things English.

The Ballymanus family had not been at Cabinteely for about ten years, and Ned had forgotten the grandeur of their great house. They were made very welcome by Robert and his wife Catherine, their arrival being half-expected, as word had come to them of Billy and Garret fighting on the United side. They sat to dinner round the long table in the dining-room, with servants waiting on them, and the silver gleaming in the candle-light. Ned was more silent than usual, being over-awed by his surroundings. He studied his host. Robert Byrne was a man of about forty, but he looked in ill-health; his face was flushed and sweaty, not with the wine, which he refused at the meal, but with some condition of the blood. His wife was fair in complexion and hair, and seemed anxious about her husband, worried that the conversation might upset him in any way; she tried to keep things at a low key. But it was not possible to avoid the talk being all of recent events, and Fanny was eager to recount their adventures. Robert Byrne did not altogether disapprove of the aims of the United Irishmen, but he was scathing about their organization, particularly since the arrests at Oliver Bond's; there seemed to be no overall plan of campaign or chain of command; the leaders had no control over their men, and the result was unco-ordinated outbreaks of violence in a variety of places which led to murders of Protestants, local revenges inflicted, massive and unnecessary destruction of property. The government, he thought, was just as bad; they too did not know what they were doing, and had no successes to report since the arrest of the Directory; they too had no control over their soldiers or their sympathizers, and this had led to all sorts of outrages against Catholics of all classes who were perfectly innocent of any active complicity in the uprising.

'No, I am wrong,' he said. 'There is one success. Lord Edward is dead.'

'Dead!' Fanny crossed herself. Lord Edward Fitzgerald was the hero of the United men, the most dashing and romantic of all the rebel leaders.

'He was caught in his hiding-place, Murphy's, the feather merchant in The Liberties. He was wounded in the scuffle, and died in prison a few days back.'

'The rebellion has no hope without him!'

'Maybe, maybe not. In Dublin they await the arrival of four huge United armies any day. I say this is nonsense. We have no signs here of rebels marching to anywhere, but, God help us, the authorities say they have news that vast numbers of well-armed rebels are moving from Meath, Kildare, and Wicklow. Dublin is in a state of siege, and no-one besieging it.'

'We have seen nothing in Wicklow of rebel armies. Garret and Billy I think are in Carlow.'

'Yes, it is nonsense, panic, wild rumours, nothing more. Here at Cabinteely we have the main road south to Wicklow and Wexford. Intelligence of both sides passes through here; I entertain commanders of all shades of opinion, and there is certainly no rebel army within a hundred miles of Dublin. The capital is strange! We are seven miles from it and it is very difficult to travel in and out; everyone is suspected of being a spy and we are stopped and searched. Loyalist troops are all round the city, an impenetrable ring I would say. Yet inside everything is as it always is—parties, balls, plays: I must tell you the other night we went to see *Robin Hood* at the Theatre Royal. Such excitement you can scarcely imagine! You could not hear the opera after the interval, the theatre was buzzing with such news. Lord Edward had been arrested that evening! Colonel Telford told me just at the end of the first act, and there was Lady Castlereagh and some of Lord Edward's cousins in the next box! What must they have thought! The viceroy himself was there; I watched him whispering incessantly with Lord Clare. But not one of them left the theatre. I suppose they thought it would not look right.'

None of the visitors knew how to keep up with such high-flying talk, and they fell increasingly silent. When dinner was finished the ladies left the room. Ned remained alone with his host. Robert refused the port, as he had refused all alcohol, but he lit a pipe.

'Catherine says it's improper to smoke, except in my library where she never goes. I say the books might get

79

burned.' He laughed. 'Help yourself to the port, Little Ned.'

'Thank you, sir.'

'You are not so little either,' Robert resumed. 'When I last saw you you were a boy of eight with dirty knees and second teeth just coming through. I told you they looked like tombstones, those teeth; do you remember?'

'Yes sir.'

'And now you are the tallest person in this house. It doesn't take long for a boy to become a man. And Ellen, what a lovely woman she has become!'

Ned thought it prudent to be non-committal. 'She's a fine, handsome girl,' he said.

'Do you see that portrait? That is Hugh O'Byrne, your great-great-grandfather. You take after him.' Ned glanced at the grave unsmiling face, then at the other pictures on the walls. He felt he was being watched by the ghosts of his ancestors, an uncomfortable sensation. What did they expect of him? The whole house made him ill at ease, the quiet servants padding purposefully to and fro, the huge expensive carpets, the high ornate ceilings and carved fireplaces. The Ballymanus family had declined in prosperity during the penal days, but at least they had not conformed, not sold out to the enemy, like Robert's forebears.

'Now', said Robert, 'there's plenty for Ellen and you to be amusing yourselves with while you are here. It's still quite safe to go out riding. How well do you shoot? There is plenty of sport here on the estate.'

'I'm sorry, but I must disappoint you, sir. I must leave early in the morning.'

'Why? How is this?' Robert frowned, and put down his pipe.

'I have to find my brothers, sir.'

'You are a United man, too? This is madness, Ned. You will stay here.'

'You are very kind but I cannot. And please, Cousin Robert, lend me one of your horses.'

'This is outrageous!' Robert rose from the table, then clutched at his temples. He was panting and seemed about to choke. He pointed at the water-jug, and fell back in his chair. Ned leapt up and rushed to him with a glass of water; Robert drank some, and recovered a little.

'It's nothing,' he said at last. 'It's the blood, only.'

'I'm sorry to be the cause.'

Robert stood up and walked with difficulty to the door. 'Take what horses you please,' he muttered. 'And leave as soon as you like. If you stay much longer it will ruin my health.'

Ned took off his shirt and lay face down on the bed. Ellen rubbed ointment into the cuts on his back. 'They are healing well,' she said. 'Do they hurt so much today?'

'Less. Ellen, I leave in the morning. Ellen, say something.'

'I can't or I'll cry.'

He turned over and pulled her down on top of him. 'I may die and I'll never know,' he whispered into her hair.

'Never know what?'

'Ellen, I can't wait, I'm saying. Not any longer.'

'We must.'

'And if I am killed, then you would spend the rest of your life knowing I was always a separate person . . . never a real part of you.'

'Ned . . . no.'

'Please.'

'No.'

The next day saw Ned riding westwards on a magnificent black horse into County Kildare. He had chosen a route through Tallaght and Rathcoole onto the Dublin-Naas road, for if the rumours proved correct then he was in friendly territory, and he thought he would find his brothers' whereabouts near Carlow, for that was where the last message from them had come. He carried with him a musket, pistols, ammunition, food, a tent, clean clothes, medicines, money and letters—one for Garret from Mary, and one for Billy from Fanny. Fanny had pestered him up till the last minute about the need to change his underclothes and the importance of finding streams in which to wash them, and the worry she would always have of him sleeping out in the open; he never threw off a cold that easily, and would assuredly catch pneumonia. His parting from Ellen had been hard to bear. His feelings were confused with desires that remained unsatisfied, fears and regrets; he still did not know what it was like, he kept thinking: for years he had wondered, four years, five years, and now he might die and never know. It would have been a mortal sin, such physical expression of their love. He wondered how this could be, but that was what the Church taught. It did not seem to him compatible with the love and compassion of Christ, but there was no getting round it. Suppose they had; suppose a bullet were then to finish him? He would go to Hell, still tainted with that mortal sin. It was a conundrum. He had not the intellect to untangle it.

At Rathcoole he was stopped and questioned by a party of men with pikes, who asked for the usual passwords; but when he replied to the question 'Where are you going to plant it?' he was corrected; the answer was 'In the crown of Ireland'. They quickly realized that Ned was one of them, and allowed him to continue, though he had to leave the

82

road and find a route back to it through a field and over two hedges, for they had blocked the way with a felled lime tree and half a dozen carts. On the far side of this barricade he saw hundreds of men drilling, cleaning pikes and guns, or just waiting. Many of them wore green cockades or hatbands. A green flag with the Irish harp flew from the upper window of an inn. Ned stopped for some ale. There was a great crowd of men inside, eager to talk. They were part of the great citizen army of Kildare, and were waiting for the signal to march on the capital.

Ned pushed his way through, accidentally jogging the arm of someone who was leaning on the counter. This man, fair-haired and red-faced, not much older than he was, nodded pleasantly, not taking any offence. He was three parts drunk. 'Dublin is ringed by ten thousand of us!' he cried, slapping Ned on the back. 'It's caught like an old fox in its den!' He swallowed his ale, some of it dripping down his chin and on to his shirt. 'Not an Englishman there has a hope of escape unless he takes to the boats!'

'We'll burn down the Castle!' another man shouted.

'And hang Lord Camden at Newgate,' said a third.

Loud cheers greeted this, and cries of 'Hanging's too good for him!'

'Give us three weeks!' the first speaker cried. 'Just give us three weeks!' He turned to Ned. 'What's your opinion, stranger? You're very silent. Where are you from?'

There was no chance, Ned thought, of any rational conversation; everyone was the worse for drink: apart from the landlord there did not seem to be a sober man in the whole tavern. 'From County Wicklow,' he said.

'Ah . . . there they're all cowards and Orangemen! Why has there been no rising in Wicklow? They've let us all down!'

'We have as yet no citizens' army.' Ned was angry, but there was no point in provoking this man. 'The garrison at Bray commands both roads to Arklow, and they've terrorized the whole countryside for miles around.'

'Ho-ho! A faint-heart!' The fair-haired man swayed unsteadily. 'We allow no cowards here! A lily-livered boy! Come outside and we'll see who's the more expert with a pike!'

Ned grabbed him by his shoulders and slowly forced him down on to his knees. The tavern fell silent, watching. Ned let him go. The man staggered upright, paid for what he had drunk and left hastily.

The others looked at Ned for a moment in silence, then turned to their own conversations. He found a glass of poteen pushed to his elbow, and the landlord said 'Are you riding towards Naas?'

'In that direction.'

'You could help me. My brother's outside, dead drunk. Would you take him home for me?'

'I will,' he answered, and swallowed the drink. He was not used to such strong waters and it hit him in the nose and behind the eyes.

'Don't venture too near to Naas,' someone warned. 'It's still in enemy hands. We've already lost a cruel number of souls there. You should be leaving that old fool by the wayside down the road.'

Ned was glad to be outside again; the inn-parlour contained too many bodies and too much smoke. The landlord picked his brother up and flung him over the horse. He gave Ned a green hat-band.

'Wear one of these and you'll not be stopped throughout the whole county,' he said. 'Leave poor Liam at the Blessington corner, just this side of Naas.'

As Ned rode on with his sleeping burden, he saw more and more men of the United army at the roadside and in the villages, mending wagons, counting pikes, celebrating. It was an impressive sight, for it was all relatively orderly, and made nonsense of Robert Byrne's sanguine opinion that there were no rebel troops surrounding Dublin. Ned thought the number of men he passed that day probably ran into thousands.

He was nearing Naas, and for a few miles now he had seen no more rebels. He took the green ribbon from his hat, fearing that a patrol of government soldiers might be venturing north of the town to learn the strength of the enemy. Poor Liam was a nuisance; he would have to be left soon. Ned had no intention of riding into Naas, not even as far as the Blessington corner. He looked for a likely side-turning that would take him well clear of the town. Liam would have to try his luck there.

Two soldiers on horseback barred his way. 'Halt!' cried one of them, pointing at Ned with a musket.

Ned did as he was told. The scene looked odd, he thought; he was dressed as a young gentleman, and the sleeping Liam's clothes were those of a labourer who had seen far better days.

'This is a poor tenant of my father's and I'm taking him to his cabin. He's blind drunk.'

It sounded so silly that he thought they must surely believe him; nobody in their right senses would make up such an absurd story. The soldiers were not interested; all they wanted was Ned's news of the rebels' movements. He told them a little of what he had seen and they let him pass. Liam was dumped like a sack of potatoes at the next crossroads and Ned galloped as hard as he could down a lane to the south-east of Naas, hoping it would be some time before the soldiers returned and found the old man.

At Kilcullen Ned experienced his first taste of real fighting. The village itself was to a large extent in ruins— roofless houses, smashed-up furniture in the street, desolation and dereliction everywhere—but this destruction was not recent, to judge by the fact that there were no fires and no corpses to be seen. The place was deserted apart from a few half-demented hairless men and women, croppies, victims of the pitch-cap. The road forked here and Ned took the turning for Carlow and New Ross. He had only gone a few yards when, on rounding a bend, he pulled sharply on the horse's reins and dismounted, for a large crowd of people were blocking the way. They were not troops of either party, but mostly women, children, and those too old to fight. They were all staring at the church which stood at the top of a hill. In the graveyard there were several hundred men armed with pikes, and, in the narrow lane leading to the church were many more similarly armed. They were not wandering about in the vague half-expectant manner of the United soldiers Ned had seen previously, but were lined up, still and tense, pikes at the ready.

From the opposite direction a shot was fired, and from beyond the crowd of spectators came the sound of galloping horses and men yelling cries of encouragement. The crowd stumbled back in Ned's direction, so he led his horse, as it was showing signs of uneasiness, into a field, and tied him to the gatepost. He loaded his musket and climbed into a tree to obtain a better view. He felt nervous and apprehensive, not because he was near the firing-line (he was well clear of it, and almost invisible in the elm leaves) but because this was the first time, the real thing, not reports and rumours and wild alarms. As he watched he was amazed to see about forty cavalrymen attempt to dash up the lane and charge the pikemen. It was the most foolish thing they could have done, and in no time at all most of them were dead or dying, horses as well as men, pierced by the terrifying pikes. The screams of the dying made Ned tremble, and to see death at first hand from a pike thrust into the heart or stomach revolted him so much that he decided then and there he could never use such a weapon. The officer leading the charge managed by skilful horsemanship and use of his cutlass to reach the graveyard, but his horse stumbled over a tombstone and threw him. His head hit another stone, and he lay there, apparently stunned; then a peasant-woman in a long black shawl ran from the church porch and stabbed him to death with a knife. Ned turned away, his stomach heaving, but he was not sick, though he wished he could be. He thought for several minutes that he would climb down from the tree when the danger was over, and ride straight back to Cabinteely. Ellen: he found he could not, try as he might, focus her face in his mind's eye; and he cursed that he had not asked her before he left for the pretty miniature that she had brought with her other possessions.

But his mood changed with the fortunes of the United men. They, foolishly, thought the battle was over when they saw the few remaining horsemen fleeing up the hill beyond the church to safety, and, giving a great cheer, they ran down to the crowd below, who were their wives and sisters, children and sweet-hearts. Some of them, as they ran and jumped over the bodies of the dead men and the carcasses of the horses threw away their pikes. There were few of them more than superficially injured by the cavalrymen's swords, and not one dead. Everyone was embracing, shouting, weeping for joy; someone started playing a violin and they began to dance in the road, raising a great cloud of dust. 'The day is ours!' they cried, and 'Did you see Eileen stab the Captain?' Ragged bare-foot children ran in and out between the dancers. Dogs dashed up and down, barking.

Suddenly there was a volley of shots and a dozen people fell to the ground. Not far from Ned a man lay on the side of the ditch, mortally wounded, blood slowly coming from his mouth. Ned stared at him with horror and fascination. The crowd scattered, screaming, in all directions, and many were saved because of the difficulty the soldiers had in seeing them clearly through the dust. The men dashed wildly back towards the churchyard, attempting to find their discarded pikes on the way, but a second, a third and a fourth volley of shots rang out and dozens of them lay dead or dying. A bullet whizzed past Ned's ear, an inch from him. His horse was whinnying in terror, pounding at the gatepost, trying to free himself. Some of the pikemen reached the church and ran inside it, or round the corners of its buttresses. The dust cleared slowly and the noise died away. Ned's horse quietened, much to his relief, for he did not want to reveal his position; for the same reason he had not fired back at the infantrymen though he longed to do so. It would have been madness, for he seemed to be the only rebel with a musket, and the direction of his shots would have been known at once.

There was a long pause. Ned could see about a hundred foot-soldiers of an English regiment. Their commander, an old man with an ear trumpet and fierce grey whiskers, addressed them with instructions to find and destroy all the discarded pikes, but what he went on to say next was astonishing. 'It is my unfortunate duty to order a retreat. The authorities in Dublin have demanded a general withdrawal of all our troops in Kildare.' There were murmurs of astonishment from the soldiers. 'We are to regroup at Naas, and if we cannot hold the town, or if there is danger of encirclement by the enemy, we are to fight our way through to Dublin. The strength of the enemy has been vastly under-estimated, and it is necessary to defend the capital at all costs.' The soldiers scattered to collect up the pikes, and when this was done they were piled up by the roadside and burned. Then they dug a pit on the side of the hill below the church and began to bury their dead. This all took a very long time, and Ned found himself growing increasingly uncomfortable on his elm-tree branch, but he dared not move. The bodies of the dead villagers and the dead horses were ignored by the soldiers, who worked unmolested, there being no sign of any wish on the part of the pikemen in and behind the church to renew the attack.

Eventually the order to fall in was given, and the retreat towards Naas began. The soldiers passed right underneath where Ned was sitting and he thought what easy targets he was being forced to miss. He was not seen by any of them; they looked dejectedly ahead of them rather than upwards. Most of them were very weary. Several noticed his horse, who was now quietly eating the grass, but none of them remarked on it. Soon they were out of sight, and the sound of tramping feet died away. Not far off a donkey began to bray and it sounded strange, as if it had been silent during the battle deliberately, and was now celebrating a return to normality.

Ned climbed down from his perch and tied the green band round his hat. He led his horse into the road where the pikemen, who had now emerged from the church, and the villagers, who had retreated into their ruined homes, were examining the bodies of their dead. A terrible lament of grief filled the air as mothers identified children and husbands recognized their wives. 'My only child!' a young woman screamed. 'Couldn't they spare my only child?' The sound gave Ned the same sense of fear and sickness that he had experienced when he had watched the cavalrymen being piked to death. Being a stranger he was questioned by several people about his movements, but nobody found his presence at all suspicious.

Despite the tragedy of the sudden death of relatives and neighbours the pikemen began to discuss their next moves, and the implications of the soldiers' withdrawal. Their leader, a young farmer, asked Ned if he would spread the news of the order for the government troops to retreat to the men in the villages along the Carlow road. Ned said he would, but he was not sure how far he was going.

'I'm looking for my brothers, both United leaders, Garret and Billy Byrne of Ballymanus.'

No-one it seemed had heard of them, until an old man thought he had heard of a Garret Byrne who had been a leader in the disastrous attack on Carlow.

'Were there many who died?' Ned asked.

'There were. They say the streets were choked with the corpses. It was a fearful slaughter.'

Ned's heart sank. 'You do not know the names of any dead?'

'No, I do not. But they weren't all killed; maybe your brothers had the luck to stay alive. They say a power of men fell back to Hacketstown, three thousand of them or more!'

'Hacketstown! That's where they were some weeks ago!'

'Ah yes, and it's many men had come from there to Carlow, and now returned there again.'

Ned rode on, forcing his tired horse at a brisk canter; the more quickly he reached Hacketstown the sooner his fears would be dispelled, but at other moments he bitterly regretted the direction his horse was taking. A pike thrust inches into his chest was a poor substitute for Ellen's kisses, and his longings for a part in freeing Ireland from her tyranny now seemed childish folly. Ellen! She was years away, yet it was only hours since he had held her in his arms. He could not remember her face in any detail at all.

A blood-red sun was sinking towards the land when Ned reached the rebel camp on a hill to the east of Hacketstown. It was still hot and would be a warm clear night. He walked into a scene of bewildering noise and bustle. At the top of the hill was an old windmill from which hung another green flag with a gold harp embroidered on it, and in large letters the words 'Liberty and Equality'. The miller, Ned was told, had long since departed with his wife and children for the comparative safety of Hacketstown, and the mill was now the rebels' main provisions store. Men seemed to be walking about inside incessantly, checking stores or helping themselves to food; from every window heads looked down on the scene, peaceful faces smoking pipes. Just outside the mill several very drunk men lay on the grass, half-empty bottles of whiskey beside them; some of them had pistols which they occasionally fired off, endangering the lives of everybody around them. The grass on the hilltop was a mass of tents, with green flags flying from the tent-poles; outside them cooking-pots hung over fires, for it was time for the evening meal, and groups of men lay on the grass, leaning on one elbow and eating from tin plates and saucepans and mugs. There were strange looted souvenirs everywhere; ten men sat to a dinner on a large carpet, springy and luxurious; another group was dining off stolen silver plate; others were dressed in fantastic clothes, looking as if they were actors in a play. Apart from the grim reminders of war—the cannon, the muskets, the stacks of pikes, swords, cutlasses, rusty billhooks and pitchforks, it could have been an enormous midsummer fair. Everyone tried to wear something green— a handkerchief, a hat-band, a dyed ostrich feather, a sash, a knitted cap—and this seemed the only thing the men, with their different accents and backgrounds, had in common; for here there was little apparent difference of class, a labourer eating round the same fire as a yeoman or a doctor or a schoolmaster.

There was a place where people were dancing, and Ned saw here for the first time that there were many women in the camp. The music—screechy fiddles—was almost inaudible in the shouting and talk and laughter, and a good many of the dancers were much the worse for drink, and tottered and fell, cursing in the foulest language as they did so. Separated from this scene by no more than a tent was a priest hearing confessions, and here orderly groups of men waited, or knelt in prayer. Further off another priest, brandishing a large plain wooden cross, was exhorting another group to flee from the wrath to come, to confess their sins and make their peace with the Lord Jesus Christ, 'for ye know not when the day may come, nor the hour.' Ned stared. The priests he had listened to at home did not preach such hell-fire and damnation; in fact they rarely preached at all, being more concerned with getting through the words of the Mass. Then he realized; this was a Protestant clergyman, a rival concern to the Catholic hearing confessions. Here, with liberty and equality, there was also religious toleration.

A girl stopped him, and said 'Hullo, Seán.'

'That is not my name,' he said, looking with surprise at the young, over-painted face. She smiled mockingly.

'Seán, Willy or Teague, it doesn't matter.'

He blushed, and knew what sort of woman she was, the

first of her kind he had ever met, and he felt ashamed of the desire that suddenly rose in him. He stumbled away, along a row of tents where women just like her sat or stood outside the entrances. 'Why so fast, handsome?' One tried to detain him, but he pushed her away roughly, and swore at her. Her laughter rang in his ears as he hurried, trying not to run, for there was no need, he thought, for him to look scared or foolish.

He passed other strange scenes. A man outside a tent was trying without much success to play a harp; he said he had stolen it in Carlow and dragged it this far, but the journey had broken many of the strings. Further on some men were carving up an ox, and stewing the pieces of it in large copper brewing-pans on a series of fires arranged in a circle. Two bald croppies played chess on a board with ivory pieces.

Eventually he came to a clearing in the middle of which was a large wooden frame; from it hung an enormous bell, and he guessed this was probably the only means of summoning this great chaotic assembly to some sort of order and organization. Beyond it was a tent, larger than most, guarded by two men with pikes. Inside shadows moved; it was now nearly dark, and whatever was going on in there was lit by many candles. One of the pikemen asked him if he wanted anything.

'I am Ned Byrne of Ballymanus, and I come seeking my brothers Garret and Billy.'

The pikeman exclaimed in astonishment, and went inside the tent. A moment later he re-emerged, Garret and Billy behind him.

'You're alive,' Ned said softly. 'You're alive!'

'Of course we are,' Garret said, his face breaking into a huge smile.

Ned tried to contain his emotions but it was impossible;

93

he ran forward and flung his arms round both his brothers.

'Ned! Ned, it's so good to see you!' Billy exclaimed, giving way to the joy he felt. 'You're well, and you look no different. Ned!'

'Of course I'm no different!' But his words were lost as Garret and Billy both spoke at once, asking how Mary and Dermot were, and Fanny and Grandfather; all three of them laughed and shouted and embraced one another so that it was impossible for a few moments to hear what each was saying.

'There are no three Irishmen as united as we are!' Billy cried.

'And we won't be separated again,' Ned answered. 'Not till the war is over.'

Garret laughed. 'We'll do our best,' he promised. 'Where is the family now? Still safe at home?'

'I stuck to my part of the bargain,' Ned said. 'I took the women to Cabinteely; I left there this morning.' His face clouded. 'Grandfather is still at Ballymanus.' And he told Garret and Billy about the arrival of the soldiers and the burning of the house. 'It's a ruin,' he said. 'And so many of our things destroyed. Your . . . I have to tell you, Billy . . . your crucifix. Garret . . . your desk, your books . . .' They stared at him, horrified and silent. 'I was tied to the triangles,' he said.

'And you survived *that*?'

'Yes, Billy.' He gently flexed his arms and his shoulder-blades; the long ride had not helped to ease the pain: he throbbed from neck to waist. 'It was only two lashes, not enough to put me out of action.' He was silent for a while, then he said 'I have letters for you. This is from Mary'—he gave it to Garret—'and this is from Fanny.'

Garret opened his at once and began to read, but Billy said

'I'll leave mine till later. You must be hungry, Ned; let me find you something to eat.' He took his brother away to one of the fires with the cooking-pots and gave him meat and wine; and while Ned ate—he suddenly realized how hungry he was, having touched nothing since breakfast-time, and he wolfed his meal down, thankfully—Billy told him what had happened since he and Garret had left for Shillelagh, years ago it seemed, but it was only weeks: what terrible loss of life had occurred among their men in the assault on Carlow.

Garret joined them. 'Mary writes that you are thinking of getting married,' he said.

Ned lit his pipe. 'I shall be nineteen soon,' he answered, 'and I won't change my mind even if I have to wait till I'm ninety!'

'You are always so emphatic!' Billy said. 'You're quite capable of arguing one week the complete opposite of what you thought last week.'

'I will do what I want. I'm man enough.'

'It's too young.'

'Oh you, I knew you'd say that, Billy!'

'The times are extraordinary,' Garret said. 'No normal considerations will ever be the same again. If you're fighting a war, you have to be adult, whatever your age may be. Do what you think is right, Ned; you have my blessing.'

'Why . . . thank you, Garret.'

'You've never known any other girl,' Billy objected.

'So Mary informed me,' Ned answered. 'She thought I should try them all out like hats in a shop. The idea has its appeal.' Garret laughed. 'But I know it's not right for me.'

'Why not wait until I'm ordained?' Billy suggested. 'I should like to be the priest at your wedding.'

'No.' Garret had given his permission, so it was pointless arguing with Billy; it was time to change the subject. He

95

told them what he had seen and heard at Kilcullen, that the government troops were making a retreat towards Dublin.

'We must tell the Council,' said Garret, scrambling to his feet. 'Come, Ned. Come and meet the leaders.'

They returned to the big tent, and Ned saw as he entered four men in officers' uniforms seated round a table, pens, papers and maps in front of them. They all looked up, wondering who the stranger might be.

'Gentlemen,' said Garret, 'I want you to meet Ned Byrne, my youngest brother, and the pride of us, Billy and myself. He is only eighteen, but as strong as I am and most of you, and as true an Irishman.'

There were welcoming voices, and a hand pushed out a chair for Ned to sit on. He was introduced to the other leaders—to Joseph Holt and Michael Dwyer, farmers, of Wicklow; to Edward Fitzgerald, whom he learned was a young farmer from New Park and no relation to Lord Edward; to a strange-looking hairless man, obviously a pitch-cap victim, who was Anthony Perry, another farmer, from Inch. Ned assumed that the four of them, like his family, belonged to that remnant of the old Catholic gentry who had managed to survive the penal days, but as soon as Anthony Perry spoke it was obvious he was an Ulsterman, and Ned was surprised to learn later that he and Holt were both Protestants, the latter with extreme radical views derived from his study of the events of the French Revolution.

Ned repeated what he had overheard at Kilcullen and there was a discussion about whether this news should alter their plans, which he learned were for an attack on the garrison at Hacketstown at dawn the following morning. Anthony Perry and Garret were for abandoning the plan and marching as swiftly as possible through the Wicklow mountains in order to provide the missing troops for the encirclement of Dublin on its southern side.

'We're lacking in arms,' said Joseph Holt, who seemed the dominant voice in this council of equals. 'If we take Hacketstown, we take with us a prodigious store of new ammunition and muskets. Perhaps many cowards will gain strength and march with us when they see our success.'

'And if we fail?'

'We will not, I think. The garrison is only a few hundred men, while we have thousands.'

'Thousands, yes!' said Garret, bitterly. 'And a more inadequate, undisciplined crowd of hobbledehoys would be hard to imagine.'

'They fight bravely. To the death at times.'

'Or waste their time stealing and burning houses; the greater part run reckless dangers and hundreds are killed quite needlessly!'

'We should be firmer. We'll give an order that anyone found looting will be hanged or shot.'

'We have done so before, and so many hundreds disobey us we can't enforce it. How can we stop them?'

Holt sighed. 'We are leaving the point,' he said. 'The question should be is it a raid on Hacketstown, or march north. Billy?'

'I'm not sure,' Billy said. 'I'll vote with the majority.'

'Hacketstown,' said Dwyer, and Fitzgerald nodded.

'If we delay much longer,' said Anthony Perry, 'the enemy will prevent us from reaching Dublin. The redcoats at Bray are holding the mountain passes, and they will soon be reinforced. If we go west of the mountains there are troops at Dunlavin and Ballymore to contend with. What do you think, Ned?'

'Me? It's not for me to say.' But the others all said he

should speak. 'The troops at Dunlavin and Ballymore will have withdrawn by now,' he said, and he sucked nervously at his pipe.

'Hacketstown,' said Holt, 'then a march through the mountains. We leave Bray to one side, and arrive at Dublin—' he peered at his map, and pointed '—here, at Dundrum. We could be there in two days.'

Garret laughed. 'We could. But our men will not.'

Billy was looking at the map. 'I agree with Joseph,' he said. 'Two days isn't long. And we need the arms.'

'Then it's decided,' said Holt. He stood up. Michael Dwyer began to blow out the candles. 'Are you happy, Garret?'

'I accept the majority, even if I disagree, just as you do, Joseph. Liberty *and* equality. Hacketstown it is.'

'You must find your brother a uniform,' said Holt, going out into the night. 'I saw a spare lieutenant's jacket in a tent somewhere.'

'I would be safer in battle in my own clothes,' Ned whispered to Billy. 'I would be less of a target for them being so tall.'

'Are you afraid then, Ned?'

'Of course I'm afraid. Aren't you?'

'Of course. All of us are. Wear ordinary clothes if you like, but I'll find you the jacket all the same, Lieutenant Byrne. You can keep it in your tent, like most of us do.'

Lieutenant Byrne! But the swelling of pride he thought he should feel did not come; it seemed easy to become a lieutenant in the United army. He was pleased, however, with the jacket; in the candle-light in Billy's tent it looked very dashing, green, with a cross on its front in silver thread. Ellen would think him a hero in it, but that sounded hollow and silly. He felt less and less as if he had the makings of a hero.

'You will be handsome in that,' said Billy, who was settling for the night on a rough and ready mattress. He pulled a blanket over himself. 'All the girls in Dublin will go weak at the knees.'

'With luck!'

'It's too late to be putting up your tent tonight, Ned. Sleep with me here; this mattress is big enough for two. It must be years since you shared a bed with me. You can rock me to sleep with talk of Mary and Dermot and Fanny.'

Ned took off his jacket and shirt and lay down beside his brother. 'I think you're safe here from a horse-whipping,' he said. Billy's laugh was muffled in the blanket. 'Dermot can now sit up,' Ned told him.

'So Fanny writes. I should love to be with them.'

'She misses you both beyond words.'

'So do I her. How's Mary?'

'More cheerful than she was.'

'She and Garret have been married only eighteen months. No wonder she was distraught when he left.'

'Why did he leave, then?'

'Because now is the time to free ourselves, and the best time there's ever been. Because life can't go on as it was. You know that.'

'Yes.'

'Where did you find that cross?' Billy fingered it.

'Ellen gave it to me.'

'The same as mine. May it protect you.'

There was a long silence. Billy turned over, and was soon asleep, his even breathing growing into a gentle snore. Ned was too excited to sleep easily. It was a very hot night, and the rough mattress itched his scars. Nor was it ever quite

99

dark; the fires that had been lit for cooking blazed on till past midnight and occasionally light would flare up as another log was thrown needlessly on to the dying flames. The noises did not fade entirely away. Dogs barked in the distance and horses stamped or coughed or whinnied from one part of the camp to another. There was a chorus of a far-off drunken song, feet passing near the tent, scraps of conversation—someone who had lost his musket and was blaming another man, a man persuading a woman to come into his tent for five minutes, a voice complaining that the whiskey had all gone. Ned tossed and turned, wishing Billy would change into Ellen. Eventually he got up and walked outside for a bit. The dew was fresh and cold on his feet. A copper-coloured full moon looked down at him. He yawned, stretched, went back to his half of the mattress, and slept.

CHAPTER FIVE

TULLOW

The attack began at eight o'clock, later than they had hoped. The rebel army drove large herds of cattle towards the town, a time-honoured practice, the aim of which was to make a protective barrier between themselves and the enemy, and, if possible, to dislodge some of the opposing soldiers from their positions. There was no possibility of surprise in the assault owing to the roaring of the animals and the inability of the rebel troops to maintain any form of discipline: many of them approached the town half-drunk, shouting blood-curdling cries and firing shots into the air like so many cowmen rounding up bullocks. The outskirts of the town were not easy to defend as there were no fortifications such as walls or a gate. There had been little attempt by the garrison to provide other than the most rudimentary barricades—most of which were pushed aside by the stampeding cattle— for they were not so much interested in saving the town as defending the barracks. The unfortunate inhabitants, whichever way their sympathies might lie, were left a prey to a marauding mob who were easily diverted from their leaders' purposes into an orgy of looting, burning, and smashing windows; though to some extent the United supporters fared better than the loyalists, and Catholics on both sides suffered less than the Protestants.

The United army came into the town from all points of the
compass. Garret had given Ned strict orders to stay with
him; he was on no account to go into any part of the place on
his own, nor to move anywhere near the front line. At first
they were both on horseback, Garret riding up and down and
urging his men on, but later they left their horses at the edge
of the town and proceeded on foot. Garret's task now was to
push his soldiers towards the barracks as quickly as possible.
Ned was sickened to see how much precious time and
energy this took; there were frequent stops to shout at men
who were trying to slip into taverns or break down the
doors of houses, and at one cottage where the door was
open, the brothers went in and Garret shot dead the
ringleader of a group of ruffians who were terrorising three
old women with threats of instant death if they did not
immediately hand over their valuables.

Ned knew that Garret had little alternative, but it
horrified him to see his brother killing a man. Garret must
have seen the look in his eyes, for he said, 'There was
nothing else I could do.'

'Yes. But I don't know if I could have done it.'

'If you think like that you had best go home. A soldier
who can't kill will soon be dead.'

'I know.'

'You're too young, Ned. I said long ago that you should
stay out of it all.'

'And you were wrong. It's taking a while to get used to;
that's all.'

At that moment there came a volley of musket-shots in
their direction. The United men ahead of them answered
with their own fire, and a gun-battle started in the street. It
appeared from this that the government troops had decided
to attack the rebels before they reached the barracks, at least,

on this, the south side of the town, a move which took Garret by surprise. In seconds the road was empty, and the only casualties appeared to be half a dozen cows, who now formed a sort of barricade, behind which a line of United men crouched and fired down the street. The rest of the soldiers found cover in alleys and doorways and kept up a continuous barrage against the enemy. Garret and Ned dodged into a house on the corner of a cross-roads and went upstairs. At the bedroom windows the owner and some other men were shooting down on the government troops. Ned recognized one of them, Thade Keogh, the blacksmith from Ballymanus, but before he could even greet him, Thade fell back, shot through the head. Ned felt weak with fright, but forced himself to the window, and aimed for the first time at another human being.

He did not keep count, but before the end of the day he had pulled the trigger hundreds of times. He was never sure whether he killed or even wounded anybody; the firing was so continuous all round him that the dead and dying could have been caused by any of the soldiers beside him. But he knew that it was probable that he had killed or maimed several. He was neither pleased nor horrified by this, but was disturbed that his emotions were so numb, that his only feeling was one of a sad remoteness from things, including his own real self. He wondered stupidly for a moment or two if he was still a human person, he who had been so pleased with his own strength and looks and arrival at manhood.

Under the pressure of the rebel musketry, which grew increasingly accurate, the government troops fell back on the barracks. The air was full of dust and acrid smoke, cries of alarm, shouted orders, the deafening thud of cannon. The day was spent running from this door to that, shots fired here or there, falling on the ground for cover, a quick glance at a dead comrade, and finally the arrival outside the barracks, where Ned and others spent hours in one place, a ditch behind a small hedge which gave them a little protection. His clothes were wet and filthy, his face smeared with dirt, and he smelled foul. There was nothing to eat. Fortunately one of his companions had a bottle of wine, and the three of them shared that; it at least took the edge off his hunger, and was not sufficient in quantity to make him careless. He had lost Garret hours ago; there had been a violent explosion, and when the dust cleared he could see his brother in a crowd of men on the other side of the street, but the chance to cross to him never occurred.

Towards five o'clock in the evening it became clear that the rebels would not take the barracks. Their casualties were heavier than those of the enemy, largely owing to the extreme daring, indeed folly, of many of their men; at times numbers of them would rush towards a cannon, or a line of musketeers, hoping to overpower them by sheer weight of numbers, and most of them ended by being blown to pieces. Suddenly, almost as if a pre-arranged signal had been given, the rebels stopped shooting. They melted from the streets, and the fire of the government troops became infrequent, then stopped. They did not give chase. One of the last bursts of gunfire came in Ned's direction. A bullet sliced a piece of flesh from his cheekbone and another hit one of his companions in the leg. He helped to pull the wounded man out of the ditch and they slowly made their way back through the alleys and narrow streets. The injured man hobbled, one arm almost strangling Ned's neck, the other round his friend's waist, and in this way, half-pulling, half-pushing him, they staggered through the silent deserted town, climbing over the bodies of the dead as they went. If they had been seen by any of the troops returning to the barracks they would have been killed instantly, but they were lucky, apart from one man they met by the church, who lunged at the wounded rebel with a long knife. Ned reacted quickly, and ran forward, knocking the man to the ground with a blow from his fist to the chin. It was the only act of violence he committed that day which brought him any sense of rightness.

At the camp on the hill there was a makeshift hospital where Ned had his cheek washed and dressed. He walked slowly to Billy's tent and dropped on to the mattress, completely exhausted. He wanted to change his clothes, wash and shave, but he was far too tired to move. His legs felt so stiff that he was not sure he could stand on his feet for long. He stared out through the entrance of the tent, down towards the town. A column of smoke rose over it from burning houses. They had gained nothing, only destroyed a great deal. It was all pointless. The sun was setting after an almost perfect day of summer heat.

Billy came in and sank down beside him.

'We are to strike camp in the morning,' he said, 'and march north to the mountains. Today has been a complete waste.'

Ned said nothing.

'Ned? I'm told you did well today. I'm told you're a born soldier. Ned? Are you all right?'

'Just totally exhausted.'

'I'll fetch you something to eat. And you should wash.' He left, and came back after a while with a bowl of soup, some bread and cheese, and a basin of hot water.

'Unbutton your jacket, Ned.'

'I can't move.'

Billy undid the jacket and Ned washed, and found himself a clean shirt.

'And will you have the power to stand it all?' Billy asked, when they had finished eating.

'Yes.'

'It's not like this every day.'

Ned stretched. His clean skin and the warmth of the food was beginning to thaw him. He filled his pipe and lit it.

'Nothing must happen to you,' Billy said. 'I love you too much.'

'More than Ireland? Is that the truth?'

'More than Ireland. You and Garret and Fanny. I wish we could all be back at Ballymanus, just as we were.'

'We could go tomorrow.'

'Impossible.'

Ned puffed at his pipe. 'Maybe I'm not so sure now about Ireland. It's a great wonder. My life was never complicated before, but some curious thing has happened today. I've ceased in some way or other to care.'

'Don't lose faith in yourself. Think of Ellen, how soon you will be together.'

'Ellen. I can't see her, not even in my mind's eye.'

'Ned, there are some days like this; there are other days. Stop thinking and sleep. Or would you like to see one of the priests?'

'No, no. I am not sick in the head.'

'I didn't mean that.' Billy sounded hurt. 'They can bring comfort, hope.'

He left soon after. Ned lay on the mattress, not bothering with the blanket as the evening was so hot. He closed his eyes, but could not sleep, though he pretended to when Billy returned. He did not sleep until long after Billy was snoring, and then shouted and twitched as he re-lived the nightmare.

108

'Garret! My horse has been stolen!'

'Have you looked for it?'

'Of course I have! Don't be a fool!' Ned was furious. 'I can't see the blasted animal anywhere!'

'I can't stop now!' Garret ran off, to argue with a group of men who were leaving the camp.

The withdrawal towards the Wicklow mountains was beginning: it was slow and chaotic, showing the same signs of poor discipline as had the attack on Hacketstown. Those who were ready first just went, without waiting for orders. The whole morning saw a thin trickle of humanity leaving the hill-top, an endless procession of carts laden with baggage of all kinds, tents, bedding, food, cooking-pots and loot. The injured, too, went on the carts, accompanied sometimes by a well-armed group of soldiers, but more often than not by one or two labourers armed only with pikes. Many of those on horseback dashed off ahead, despite the desperate pleas of the leaders for them to stay and guard the carts and the walking wounded, who would be an easy prey to any detachment of government troops.

The Hacketstown garrison was not slow to take advantage of this and attacked the column all day long. Despite their success in defending the barracks yesterday they were still greatly outnumbered by the rebels, so these skirmishes were small affairs and caused little loss to the rebels' carts, and none to their horsemen; but those who hobbled or walked on crutches were picked off mercilessly.

Ned wasted a great deal of time searching for his horse; it was nowhere to be found. It was almost certainly by then carrying one of the more cowardly rebels over the Wicklow border. He cursed his luck, realizing that all he could do now was to walk. He was one of the last to leave the hill, and armed with a musket he trudged along beside a cart for

109

hours, talking with a soldier who had lost both arms in the action outside the barracks. Although this man was in great pain he was extraordinarily cheerful, and the time passed not too unpleasantly for Ned, whose only immediate troubles were the stiffness in his legs, and the choking dust that so many feet and wheels and another very hot summer day were causing.

The road passed over a bridge where the fields ceased and the heather and bogs of Wicklow moorland began, and suddenly they were fired on by half a dozen government cavalrymen, who rode off as quickly as they had appeared when two well-aimed rebel shots killed two of them, and a third brought down one of their horses. The dismounted rider, instead of lying flat, or running for cover, charged straight at Ned, and knocked the musket out of his hand with a pike. Ned was so taken by surprise that he did not stoop to pick up the gun, though he had time to do so, but ran to the cart, thinking the soldier was mad, and seized a pike to defend himself with. The soldier charged again, but Ned was the quicker and had the longer weapon, and, with a sense of nausea, he felt it stick a foot or more inside his enemy's stomach. The soldier fell back so heavily that the pike was wrenched out of Ned's hands, and he disappeared head over heels, over the parapet of the bridge and onto the river bank, where the force of his fall pushed the steel right through him.

Ned, horrified at what he had done, rushed down the bank. The driver of the cart shouted 'Come back! Come back!' but he took no notice. Blood was pouring from the injured man's wounds and from his mouth and nose, but he was still alive, and writhing in pain. He was trying to speak. He was a boy no older than Ned.

Ned cried out in anguish 'Why did you make me do it?'

The boy whispered something inaudible, and Ned knelt down beside him.

'Finish it,' he said hoarsely.

'I can't!'

'Please.'

Ned looked at his eyes, transfixed by the intensity of the gaze on the young face, but he forced himself to look away. 'You're forcing me to . . . into damnation,' he said.

'Bastard.' The whisper was slower, but he forced the words out with great difficulty. 'Irish bastard.'

Ned took out his pistol and shot him in the head.

Evening found him near the rebel camp in the mountains, not many miles from his home. He could not remember how he arrived there. All day he had tramped on with unseeing eyes, in a state of acute torment and distress. He had thrown his pistol onto the cart and walked weaponless. If government soldiers had appeared he would gladly have allowed himself to be shot. It was a punishment just to be alive. He felt his whole being was stained for ever; there was no way conceivable of washing this terrible sin out of him. He was damned. Not in a doctrinal sense; a priest sympathetic to the United cause would give him an easy absolution, would indeed wonder what kind of sin this was he had come to confess, when it was a holy thing to rid Ireland of her oppressors. It was much worse than that: he had condemned himself; he was not fit to live; no human being guilty of what he had done that day had any human rights or attributes any longer. There could never be any possibility of a return to normality, to life at home at Ballymanus, or marrying Ellen. Ellen—he would never see her again, not in any circumstances; he was not worth the mud in her cottage doorway. He remembered the cross round his neck, and

111

wrenched it off and threw it, as far as he could hurl it, into the heather.

As he entered the camp he passed the same woman who had accosted him on the hill at Hacketstown.

'Are you coming in, Seán?' she asked.

Despite the pain in his mind he felt the same sudden desire in his body as last time, and thinking it did not matter now, nothing mattered any more, he followed her. As they were walking towards her tent they saw Billy approaching. Ned wished the ground would open and swallow him up.

Billy stopped, and looked at him, amazed. 'What do you think you're doing?'

'Go away,' said Ned, wearily.

'God spare us!' Billy did not try to contain his anger. 'Oh, we were wrong to let you leave home! We've failed in ourselves and in our duty to our parents, God rest their souls! This . . . *thing*! Have you no shame?'

'So it's you, Billy Byrne,' the girl said. 'I thought I remembered the sound of your voice.'

'So you know her?' Ned asked.

Billy almost struck him. 'I do not know her! Not in the way you mean! This piece of *filth* is Biddy Doyle; her father worked for us until we turned him off for stealing. Surely you remember?'

'You never told me.'

'So this is your brother, Billy Byrne. He looks twice the man you are!' She laughed in his face.

'If I see you near Ned again I'll have you tied to a post and whipped!'

'You'll surely be sorry you were saying that, Billy Byrne,' she shouted. 'You'll rue the day you said that!'

Billy pulled Ned away with him. 'If you dare to think that

112

I've ever been with her, or any other woman, strong though you think you are, I'll thrash you too!'

Ned broke free from his grip and walked off. He walked for hours. It was long after dark when he began to wonder where he could sleep. He had no idea where his own tent was, and he did not feel worthy of sharing Billy's mattress. He lay down at last in the heather and slept under the stars.

The camp was attacked by a force of government soldiers at breakfast-time the following morning. The rebels, taken completely by surprise, scattered in all directions. Ned, weaponless and still in the depths of despair, quietly surrendered. He expected to be shot, but this contingent of troops displayed unusual humanity, and instead of the massive slaughter they could have inflicted, contented themselves with firing only at those who were escaping, and marched back towards Hacketstown with a large number of prisoners. Ned plodded along the whole length of the road he had travelled yesterday, hands tied firmly behind his back. He felt sick as they approached the bridge where he had piked the English boy, and he noticed, with a shudder, that the body was still lying on the river bank.

They marched through Hacketstown and on to Tullow where they were locked up in the gaol. Ned found himself in a small cell with a dozen other men, all of them young. The eldest he discovered later was only twenty-two, and he wondered if prisoners had been put, for some strange reason, into separate age groups. The soldiers beat some of them with their muskets, then left them to their own devices, though ten minutes later the door was thrown open, and another man, screaming oaths and protests, was pushed inside.

First words among the prisoners were of escape, but it

was obviously impossible. There was one window, quite large, high up in the wall, firmly barred. Ned, the tallest man there, allowed another prisoner to climb onto his shoulders and test the bars, but they did not budge at all.

The cell was totally bare, except for some straw in one corner. Shouts, blows on the door brought no answer from outside. Nothing happened for several hours. Eventually the door was unlocked, and a turnkey entered, escorted by a party of armed soldiers. He carried a plate of potatoes which he left on the floor. All the inmates had to share this, and eat lying down, their mouths to the plate, for their hands were still bound.

'You're taking more than you should, you bastard!' a man shouted at Ned.

'I am not! Bastard yourself!'

The man kicked at him, and Ned kicked back. Relationships which had begun to blossom suddenly turned sour as they all found themselves very hungry. The meal was punctuated by blows and groans, curses and insults.

Nothing happened for days. The only times the door was opened were when the turnkey brought food, or soldiers came to order the prisoners to take out the straw, which was soiled with excrement, and put down fresh. They became like animals. They fought all the time over the food, trying to take advantage of Ned at first as he was the youngest, but soon learning to respect the power of his boots. They got used to the foul stench of each other's bodies, and bodily functions. They had no means of washing and their skin itched. Ned found lice in his hair and on his body. Their beards grew. At night they slept on the floor, bothered at times by rats. At first there had been the beginnings of friendships, the exchange of news about the war, stories of battles they had seen, miraculous escapes and unendurable

114

hardships. But the fights over the food, the whole routine of their existence, prevented any goodness in them coming to the surface; after a week they became sullen and uncommunicative, living only to the promptings of the body; hunger, sleep, defecation.

One morning a new prisoner, Michael Donnelly, was thrust in among them. He brought them the surprising news that the rebellion was collapsing on all sides. In County Wexford, where it had been most successful, General Lake's troops were inflicting a campaign of brutal savagery on the people, and in Wexford City, which had been for a month the headquarters of the republic, the red white and blue once again fluttered from every flagpole. In Ulster there had been a major uprising, but that too had been crushed. The vast army of United men surrounding Dublin had been dispersed. Only in Wicklow was there any serious resistance still. The defeated army of Hacketstown, now much smaller in numbers because of massive desertions, was hiding in the wilds of Glenmalure, occasionally making surprise raids on the troops. It was safe in the almost impregnable mountain fastnesses. Michael Donnelly's audience greeted the news with words of despair and useless demands for revenge; only Ned was silent.

'We are all to be court-martialled,' Michael said. 'The hearings begin this morning. They were not started earlier because the garrison has been too busy chasing the rebels into the mountains.'

'Who is to preside at the trials?' someone asked.

'General Dundas.'

'What is he like?'

'Unpredictable. Sometimes it's shooting or hanging, but if he thinks you have useful information he orders a flogging. But there's a bright side . . . many he's set free.'

115

One after the other they were taken from the cell. The first, John Kinsella, a fair-haired man from Kilkenny, was flogged. The others had no idea what the nature of his offence was, but he had been the least violent and vicious of the group. They heard the sound of the lashes out in the yard, and stood on each other's shoulders to look through the barred window. He was stripped to the waist and bound to the triangles. Ned watched first: the man cried out incessantly with the pain, but he did not offer to talk; after the twentieth lash he appeared to faint. Ned climbed down, sickened at the sight of the blood and the raw tender flesh, and felt momentarily glad that his despair had not destroyed all his capacity to feel sorrow and disgust. At last the sound of the whip stopped, and Ned climbed up a second time; the man was dead, his spine clearly visible where the flesh had been torn away.

Ned was last to go, except for Michael Donnelly. He was led to a room where three officers sat behind a desk. In the middle sat the general, a sad-faced elderly man, who conducted the proceedings.

'Name?'

'Ned Byrne.'

'Occupation?'

'Gentleman.'

The three officers looked at him, surprised.

'Age?'

'Nineteen. I'm nineteen this day,' he added, suddenly remembering.

'You look older. The beard. Are you related to Garret Byrne of Ballymanus?'

'No.'

'How long have you been fighting in the rebel army?'

'Two days, when I was captured.'

116

'Where do you live?'

'Nowhere.'

'Nowhere? That is a silly answer. Where do you live?'

Silence.

'I suppose you saw John Kinsella being flogged? That will soon make you tell us.'

'He didn't speak.'

'But you are younger, not used to pain.'

'You may try it if that is your wish.'

They looked at him in amazement.

'Don't tempt me too far.'

Ned guessed then that the general had no intention of flogging him, which was confirmed when the officer on his left said, 'I suggest a hundred lashes,' and the general dismissed the idea with a wave of his hand.

'Your courage is foolish,' said the general. 'Who are you?'

'Tell me if I'm to be shot or hanged or flogged. It makes no difference to me.'

'Why?'

'Because—'. He stopped, deciding it was no concern of theirs what his state of mind was.

The general sighed. 'I heard three weeks ago that my only son is dead, piked somewhere near Hacketstown. He was nineteen; he looked not unlike you. Isn't it time all this finished?'

'Yes.'

'We have nothing against you, Ned Byrne. You won't suffer, if you just answer a few questions.'

'I'll not be answering your questions.'

The general sighed again. 'Lock him up. We'll talk to him another time.'

'A few lashes, sir, would save a lot of trouble, if I might say so with respect,' said the officer who had spoken before.

117

'Be quiet, lieutenant. You do not say so with respect. Take this boy out.'

Ned was taken to another cell, a much smaller place with very little light, damp and draughty, quite different from the muggy warmth and human stench of his former prison. He was there for five days. He longed for something different to eat, even if it was only a crust of bread; potatoes and water had been his only food since he had been imprisoned. He was permanently hungry, and beginning to feel a little weak.

But the five days' solitude was good for him. Very slowly his mind began to heal. He could not bear to entertain the mental image of how he had killed the boy on the bridge, and he shut it out every time his thoughts wandered near to it, nor could he even dream of it at night. So that boy was probably General Dundas' son. What nightmares did the general suffer as a result? His own frequent nightmare was re-living the march towards the bridge and some other kind of violence—an explosion, musket-fire from an ambush— always stopped him reaching it. But as he lay on the floor, or sat, or stood and studied the pattern of cracks in the wall, he began to feel the shock flowing gradually out of him and he thought that it might be possible to forgive himself. This was not to be achieved, he began to see, by his own death, or by the mutilation of his own body in a flogging, or brutish coupling with a whore; for this, too, he realized, would have been, if he had done so, a kind of self-inflicted wound. His natural instincts were to expiate one act of violence with others against himself, but they were no expiation. For a long time the act of absolution was vague and formless. He turned ideas over endlessly in his mind. Once he had admitted the chance of forgiveness, his brain raced to find the way. It would have something to do with never touching any kind of weapon again, not even to shoot at a

118

rabbit; certainly, should he be freed, never to re-join the United army; perhaps leaving Ireland, which would always be a tainted place now, and going somewhere into exile. And Ellen? If he forgave himself, would she forgive him? Perhaps, one day, far off, he would be so far restored to himself that they could marry. And once he had allowed himself to think of her as a possibility, she flooded back into his mind; he relived all the memories of their relationship with a new tenderness: he could even see her. He found he was weeping uncontrollably.

He went before Dundas again.

'Are you Garret Byrne's brother?'

'No.'

'You live at Ballymanus?'

'No.'

'We don't believe you.' Silence. 'Very well. You may as well know his little band up in the mountains is still giving us a great deal of trouble. They have even kidnapped one of our officers. I have sent messages to them that I am willing to exchange you for Colonel Telford. Of course if they execute him I shall execute you. I think your brother understands that all right. Whatever happens, the rebels will lose in the end, and I shall see myself to your brother's trial, which can only end in his being hanged. Do you have anything to say?'

'No.'

General Dundas became more conciliatory. 'Drop all this stubbornness, Ned Byrne. Why not speak now? Tell us all you know. Why not join our side? You're strong and manly. You'd make a good soldier.'

Ned's lip curled in contempt.

'I see. You say you are a gentleman and I believe you. You're Garret's brother. We shall now treat you like a gentleman. The English are not all brutes. Take him away to his room.'

It was on the top floor. There were, it was true, bars on the window, and an impossible jump to the ground, and the door was always kept locked, but there was a bed with a mattress, blankets and clean linen; a table and a chair; a wardrobe; a bookcase full of books; paper and writing materials. He was allowed a hot bath. His clothes were taken away, and a new coat, shirts, and knee-breeches sent in to him. He was given three good meals a day. He had no idea why he was being treated with such kindness; it was certainly not just because Garret had captured Colonel Telford. The colonel was probably having a very rough time in the open air up in the mountains. The only explanation he could think of was that it was done on the orders of General Dundas, who must, presumably, be paying for the food and clothes; perhaps he, too, needed to make some kind of atonement, for his dead son. Ned's jailer was a young officer, Tom Austen, not much older than himself, who sat with him in his spare time and talked and played chess. He came from a similar background to Ned; his father owned a small estate in Devon and he had a brother who was a curate. He was himself the youngest son, and had joined the army to seek his fortune. They exchanged confidences. Ned admitted to him that Garret was his brother. He occasionally brought Ned a bottle of wine, and lent him a pipe and tobacco.

He spent two months in that room. The negotiations over Colonel Telford were complex and protracted. Ned was told how things had progressed, how long a time it took to convince Garret that General Dundas had really imprisoned him; how on one occasion the representatives of each side had been killed on the journey; or how Garret was dicing with his life, attempting to obtain a free pardon for the leaders as part of the bargain. General Dundas eventually lost patience and informed Ned that he had told Garret that unless Colonel Telford arrived in Tullow at noon in three days' time he would be hanged.

Ned did not answer immediately. 'I think that is bluff,' he said at last.

The general smiled. 'You won't think so when you're taken out to the scaffold!'

Ned shook his head. 'I'm not so sure that you really want me to die.'

'You're just a pawn in the game, nothing else. Quite dispensible, if necessary.'

Did Dundas really mean that, Ned asked himself. No: it was bluff. 'It's not lost on me that you treat me much better than I deserve,' he said.

'Our usual methods may win wars. But they don't win hearts.'

'That's not it. You said . . . I reminded you of your son.'

'He was the same age. And just about as stubborn.'

'I don't want to talk about him.'

'Why not?'

Ned did not answer. If the boy he had piked on the bridge was in fact General Dundas' son; if he admitted that he was responsible, what would his position be then? He had a curious urge to tell all, but he knew that if he did so he would be signing his own death warrant.

'You're a strange man,' the general said.

He obviously wished in these interviews to make human contact, perhaps to strike some kind of bargain; but Ned always remained polite and formal, despite Dundas appearing to be almost fond of him. He felt very sorry for Dundas.

Tom Austen brought him the news. The rebellion was over, except for the guerilla bands like Garret's in the mountains. Then there was excitement over the landing of the French who arrived at last, at Killala, their rapid advance across the country, the ignominious defeat of General Lake's army at Castlebar ('It surely could not have happened to a more suitable fellow,' Ned murmured, and Tom did not disagree), and their final surrender to Lord Cornwallis at Ballinamuck a month later. Ned listened to the tales of this strange invasion with detached curiosity. If only it had occurred months earlier, the course of the rebellion might have been very different. But he no longer cared.

He watched the hot dry summer change to autumn. The unusual heatwave broke; wind and wet returned. He listened with a kind of comfort to the rain drumming on the roof and the gales shaking the trees; the yellow leaves whirling in the wind, the gusts rattling the window and slamming distant doors suited his sad resigned mood. For though this weather brought the pleasure of the familiar landscape of his home to his mind, he had resolved, if he was freed, to leave Ireland. Hope was restored to him; a new place, a new life. The healing process was almost complete.

He was never allowed out for exercise, and he kept himself fit by walking round and round his room, and doing physical exercises on the floor. He kept his arm muscles in trim by pulling at the window-bars, but they never gave. He could think of no other method of escape, unless he murdered Tom Austen, and though his thoughts frequently led him to devise all sorts of plans for making his way out of the barracks he never put any of them into action. Much of the time passed in thoughts of Ellen. He wrote long passionate letters to her, telling her what had happened; he omitted nothing, forcing himself to write of the poor piked soldier, his encounter with the woman. But as there was no way of sending them he tore them up.

Late one evening he was disturbed by the noise of gunfire, very close at hand, and running feet in the corridor. There were more shots and the cries of wounded men. The key turned in the lock and the door burst open. It was Garret.

'Ned! Thank God!' He pulled Ned from the room and along the corridor, where they passed Tom Austen who was on his back on the floor, dying. The musket-fire was continuous and deafening as they raced down the stairs and out to freedom. Garret pointed to a horse and Ned, needing no second bidding, leaped on to it and galloped away. A hail of bullets followed them. It was the same coal-black horse Ned had ridden from Cabinteely.

'Success! Total success!' Garret shouted as they rode out of Tullow. 'And we still have Colonel Telford!'

They stopped their horses in a clump of trees, and waited for the rest of the United men to catch up with them. They soon arrived, twenty of them; there were no injuries apart from three or four slight flesh wounds. Men Ned vaguely recognized shook his hand, slapped him on the back, asked him a dozen questions.

The raid had taken Dundas completely by surprise. He was expecting a rescue attempt in the early stages of his negotiations with Garret, but had miscalculated with his ultimatum, imagining it would bring only Colonel Telford to Tullow, not twenty fearless hard-bitten rebel soldiers on horseback. Apart from Tom Austen, three other Englishmen had died in the raid.

123

'How's Billy?' Ned asked.

'I haven't seen him for a week. He's with a party of men in the hills near Wicklow. But . . . just you wait till Ellen sees you!'

'Ellen?'

'She's with us, in the camp.'

Ned's heart turned over. 'How, Garret, how?'

'I sent a message by Dan Carty, one of our most trusted men, to tell her you were taken prisoner. He slipped through the enemy lines and soon reached Cabinteely. She begged him to take her back with him, and the fool has a soft heart with women in tears. I threatened to send her straight home, but I'm a fool also. She's been worried out of her wits these past five weeks. You've certainly made her love you.'

'Does her mother know?'

'I had to be risking Dan Carty's life again with another message.'

Ned, weak though he felt from his months in prison, spurred on his horse and rode like the wind towards the wilds of Glenmalure.

CHAPTER SIX

BALLYMANUS

The October morning was bright and cold. They walked away from the camp, hand in hand, the flame-coloured ferns crackling like dead leaves underfoot. All around the mountain peaks soared, dissolving in the distance in a wash of colour, the purple heather and white granite merging in the brilliance of the low sun into a soft dream-like landscape. Some crows flapped upwards from a dead sheep, like blackened paper rising from a fire. Otherwise there was no movement. A horse in the camp neighed; another answered and a dog barked. They looked down at the narrow track in the valley leading to civilization, to the enemy. Ahead the huge summit of Lugnaquilla reared up, an impenetrable barrier between the rebels and the government troops. It was the most remote, the safest hide-out the rebels could have found.

Ned and Ellen sat on the mountainside against a boulder, huddling together for warmth under Joseph Holt's greatcoat. He told her everything that had happened.

'It alters nothing,' she said.

'It was a vast mistake, going in the first place. I'm sorry.'

'Stop being sorry! You hurt your own self far more than me. Poor Ned. But you're still Ned.'

'The cross.'

'It's nothing.'

'It is.'

She stood up and held out her hand to him. 'We should go and see Father Malone.'

'Why? I don't want to go to confession yet, or the sacraments. I'm not ready.'

'I didn't mean that.'

He realized. 'Ellen! *Today?*'

'Why not?'

He kissed her. 'Your mother.'

'Yes. Now I'm sorry. But it isn't as it should be, the way we have to live now.'

Ned told his brother, and added that if Garret would give them horses he and Ellen would leave the camp immediately afterwards, and go first to Ballymanus, then, when it was possible, attempt to find a ship that would take them to France. Garret tried to dissuade him. It was too dangerous; General Moore's troops were at the bottom of Glenmalure, trapping their way out. But Ned was insistent, saying they would cross the mountain peaks, and Garret gave in, realizing that his younger brother had gained in the last few months an authority that was impossible to deflect.

'We may never see each other again,' Garret said. 'This war has surely ended in ruin for us all.'

'Why not surrender, Garret?'

'No, never. We cannot now.'

'What will you do in the winter? You'll freeze to death in the frosty nights and the snow.'

'We'll disperse and make our way separately over the mountains. We still have friends who will give us sanctuary. You see we are not many now; it would not be too difficult.'

128

It was true; there were very few tents compared with the enormous encampment on the hill at Hacketstown. The band of three thousand United men now numbered about fifty.

'We will find ways of keeping in touch.'

'We may break out of here yet. These are the best men left to us, palace guards, hard as flint, and devoted yet to the cause. We could give General Moore a good beating with the help of God and a little luck. And if we did, others who are now lying low would join us.'

'I wish you were not, Garret.'

'What?'

'Devoted yet to the cause.'

The tent was dark inside and it was a few moments before Ned could see Colonel Telford properly. He was bound hand and foot. He was much younger than Ned had imagined, a bullet-headed man with close-cropped hair, his gaze hard and penetrating, the blue eyes fierce.

'Who are you?'

'Ned Byrne.'

'I thought so. I look forward to the day when I shall see you dangling from the end of a noose.'

'I've done nothing to harm you. I came to ask if you would like a smoke.'

'Thank you.' Ned placed his pipe between the colonel's teeth and lit the tobacco with a twig from the camp fire. 'Is that all you came for?' the colonel asked.

'I'll be leaving here today for my home. I was wondering if I could do anything, take a message to your wife.'

'How can you do that? Why do you want to?'

'I don't know how, but I'll try. Why is it I want to? Because I belong to neither side, not any more. I hope I shall never fire a shot at another man again! And I hope I shall never clap eyes on a pike.' He shuddered. 'And I can't bear to see a man caged up as you are. I'd cut that rope if I dared.'

'They treat me well enough. I'm only tied up like this when there's no one free to guard me.'

'Is your wife in Dublin?'

'Yes. But you would not dare to go there.'

'I will try through my cousins at Cabinteely.'

Ned pushed back the tent flaps, and looked out.

'Why don't you dare to untie these ropes? Your reward would be very considerable.'

Ned smiled. 'I could not.'

'No.' The colonel sighed. 'Take your pipe.'

'You may keep it.'

'Take it from my mouth then. It will be a reminder of an odd conversation.' The colonel struggled nearer to Ned. 'Tell her how much I love her . . . I love her so much. And that I'm fit and well, and'—his voice shook a little—'that I shall see her soon. I hope.'

The wedding was delayed until the afternoon as Garret and Father Malone were away down the valley with several other men looking for supplies. A village some miles away gave the rebels meat, eggs and vegetables. The people there were risking their lives and the destruction of their property, but the United dream still lived in their hearts.

Garret gave Ellen to Ned. Joseph Holt and Anthony Perry were the witnesses. The ceremony was in the open air, between the tents, in the warm hazy sunlight.

He turned on to his back, and peered out under the tent. Their two horses, turned loose, were munching the moun-

130

tain grass. There was a frost. The October sky blazed with stars.

He wriggled down, pulling her against him, under a heap of blankets, clothes and rugs.

'What is it?' she whispered.

'Nothing.'

'My soft cheek. Your rough cheek.'

'I had a beard at Tullow. I forgot to tell you.'

'What was it like?'

'Thick. Curly. It gave me the shock of a lifetime to look in a mirror and see it. It was so black.'

'A part of you I will never be knowing.'

'I'll grow another for you.'

'No. I mean the prison, the life you led.'

'I'll not live that again. Destroying myself. What goodness I have all destroyed.'

'Not destroyed. It grew again. You're a better person.'

'I am not.'

'What should we call our son?'

He laughed. 'They'll not come as quickly as that.'

'I know.'

'Garret. The eldest boy has always been Garret.'

'I have no choice?'

'No.'

'Then there must be two. Another Little Ned.'

'One isn't enough for you?'

'One Ned or one baby? I want six.'

'And you an old hag after.'

'Shall we sleep?'

'No.'

'I love you.'

'I love you.'

131

The sun was high when they woke. Ned was out first; the air was bitterly cold after the heat of their bodies under the blankets. A thin dusting of snow lay on the grass, dazzling in the brilliant sunlight. The ashes from last night's fire were dead. He dressed quickly, and ran about to get warm. The mountain peaks watched him, range on range, disappearing under the curve of the sky in all directions, Lugnaquilla still clearly the highest, but far away now to the north. The horses whinnied and climbed up to him. He stroked and patted them, and they nuzzled against his face. Ellen came out of the tent, shivering.

'Shall I light the fire?'

'No, we should saddle the horses and go. We can be home by mid-afternoon and eat in the warmth.'

'If anyone is there. If it's still standing.'

'We'll manage. Come and kiss me.'

She put her arms round him. 'My Ned,' she murmured sleepily.

'Should we be going back inside?'

'No.'

'Why not?'

'You said we should saddle the horses and go.'

It was a long slow climb up to the top, leading the horses all the way. The snow was very little, but it was melting, and the horses kept slipping. The other side of the mountain was steep and stony, enormous boulders littering the slope. Below them were acres of purple heather and in the bottom a wide sluggish river; on the far side a few sheep in the grass and ferns, and above that another mountain, its heather a reddish brown in the distance. There was no obvious path. The horses found it very difficult and had to be led all the way. As they rested underneath a boulder Ned saw red dots moving up the valley far away to their left.

132

'Redcoats.'

'What shall we do?'

'Wait.'

The soldiers were moving along the river bank, thirty of them, spread out haphazardly. They did not see Ned and Ellen, high up near the summit. In time they disappeared from view, towards the top of the valley.

'What are they doing?'

'Probably trying to surprise poor Garret from behind. Though they'll have to struggle over the top of Lugnaquilla to do so.'

'Should we go back and warn him?'

'We wouldn't get there in time, I'm afraid.'

Ned waded through the river with the horses. It was icy cold and came up to his waist. Then he returned and carried Ellen across. She urged him to take off his wet clothes and wait for them to dry, but he would not. They dragged the horses up through the heather, another slow exhausting climb. At the top there was another similar descent, then upwards again. They dared not go down any of the valleys for fear of General Moore's troops, but they longed to do so. Each ascent and drop had its own difficulties: on one slope there was a huge expanse of gorse, beautiful in its autumn yellow, but murderous to find a way through; on another there were old peat cuttings, treacherously covered by new heather, easy to fall into unawares and break a leg. It became obvious eventually that they would not get home that day, and at nightfall they camped half-way up another towering mountainside on the edge of a wood. These were the only trees they had seen all day, apart from a few solitary rowans, their scarlet fruit brilliant against fading grey leaves; but these were firs, a gloomy dark green, whispering incessantly. Ned thought it must be a plantation, and was

133

worried that they might be a little too close to a house. But he was too exhausted to go on. They erected the tent and lit a fire; Ellen cooked, and Ned sprawled out near the flames. His damp clothes he hung up to dry in the heat.

He shivered against her under the blankets, a little feverish.

'You should have changed as soon as we crossed the river. If you're really sick, what should we do?'

'I'll survive.'

'Ned.'

'Mmm.'

'We have no wedding ring.'

'Does it matter?'

'Yes.'

'I shall give you my mother's when we see Fanny. She has it with her, at Cabinteely.'

'What is it like?'

'Very old. Very beautiful.'

'Listen to the trees.'

'Like voices.'

'I wish my mother knew.'

'Garret will send Dan Carty, and she will surely know by now.'

'Do you love me?'

'So much it hurts, it aches.'

'That's the sickness. You're very hot.'

All night the trees rustled and Ned, in a feverish half-sleep heard them as if they were the blood rushing inside him, restless yet soothing, his fever part of his happiness, the flimsy tent and the firs a protection against the vastness of sky and landscape outside, the great boulders and immense distances of the mountains present in his eyes all night, his arms round Ellen, her breath on the skin of his chest and throat, and nothing else, nothing, ever being of such importance ever again as the face of her, trustingly asleep.

Next morning the frost was thicker, crystals sparkling on every surface. The ground was hard. Ned, very feverish, did not notice the cold, but he suffered a great deal on the journey up the mountain. The rocks moved and swayed round him and he stumbled and fell several times. Looking back into the valley made him dizzy, and the fir plantation, almost black against the green background, was a threatening ever-moving shape, trying to catch them and swallow them up. He rested, sweating, teeth chattering. Ellen led her horse to the top and came back for his.

'We are nearly there,' she said. 'This is the last; on the other side the land is flat.'

At the top, he thought all Leinster lay below him. They could see far into Carlow and Wexford. There were fields and farms, distant towns; somewhere, quite near, was Ballymanus; and away, the sea near Waterford, the edge of Ireland. The weather was changing. The wind was a little stronger, and in the south-west slate-coloured clouds were piling up on the horizon. At the bottom there was a good road, and they were able to ride the horses for the first time since they left the camp in Glenmalure. Ned clutched tightly onto the reins, the motion of the animal making him sick, his eyes unable to focus on anything. Several times he nearly fell off.

The soldiers were right in front of them as they rounded a bend. Ned's heart leaped in fear, but he need not have worried. The lieutenant was polite, not very interested in them, did not even ask where they had come from.

'My husband is sick,' said Ellen. 'Please do not trouble him.'

One glance at Ned showed this to be true. Had they, the

135

officer asked, heard any news or rumours about the rebels in the mountains?

'No, nothing. It is surely quiet where we are in Kiltegan. We have not seen or heard them.'

The lieutenant was satisfied and the soldiers left them; Ned wondered vaguely where he had seen the man's face before, and as they rode through Hacketstown, still ruined but now at peace, he realized that the soldiers were from the garrison there, and that he had fired a dozen times at that officer from the upper window of the house where Thade Keogh was shot.

At Ballymanus the war had clearly disturbed the rhythm of the year on the farm; the corn had not all been cut; in two fields the stooks had not been carted, and the usual stubble of October made only one yellow square on the hillside. Someone was ploughing in the wasted barley, two horses plodding slowly along the hedge, brown earth turned neatly over in lines behind them. But the house astonished him. Ned expected to find the same half-ruin he had left, but Grandfather and his friends had certainly been busy. The top storey had been completely demolished, and a new roof had replaced it, of slate. It made the house look very long and squat, less warm than the friendly slope of thatch, but there was no doubt it was neat and smart, a cheering proof that the summer and autumn of that year had not been seasons entirely of destruction.

The door was open, but there was nobody at home. All the broken glass, the torn pictures and the smashed furniture had been removed; everywhere there was order and cleanliness. Ned went straight to bed, not in his old room, but in the double bed in Garret's room. Ellen made him a hot drink and warmed bricks to put under the blankets. His face was ashen. Very soon he slept. He woke, hours later in the dark, to feel Ellen asleep beside him, then slept again, waking in full daylight to find he was alone in bed, with a grey mild day outside, wind in the monkey-puzzles and gentle rain on the window's new glass.

The door opened. It was Grandfather.

'You've slept many long hours,' he said, as calmly as if they'd last seen each other yesterday. 'And you are not to get up. Ellen has said.' And he went.

Ned dressed slowly. The fever had gone, but he felt weak. He sat downstairs in the armchair in front of the kitchen fire, happily absorbing the heat. Grandfather sat on the other side, beaming with pleasure.

'My chair. Your father's chair, then Garret's. Now it's yours. You're master, for the present, till Garret comes home.'

'How are you, old man?'

'We've worked hard. You can see that. There was plenty to do.'

'Ellen's told you?'

'Yes, my Little Ned. A married man! I'm glad I've lived to see it, whatever else has happened, or may happen.'

Ned smiled. 'I'm happy. We both are.'

'Why not? And were you a good soldier? A crack shot? Ah . . . you'll have been a credit to the Byrnes.'

'I don't want to talk about it. I've seen horrors.'

'So Ellen's told me.'

'Everything?'

'Yes.'

Ned sighed. 'Then there's no more to say.'

'There's a lot more to say,' Grandfather said, and he stood up. 'I've work for you. You're the master now. There's men to be paid, and a sale to be thought of for the wheat, and decisions to make about selling calves. There's some should be sold. Tomorrow, when you're stronger. And you can shoot me some pheasants in the copse. I'm partial to pheasant. I can't shoot so well now; this autumn's brought me rheumatism.'

'I'll never be handling a gun in my life again.'

'Nonsense!'

'And we shan't stop long. I'm thinking of leaving for France, as soon as it's possible.'

'And what should happen to me, and to Fanny, and to this house? I've not done all this work for no purpose. If Garret and Billy never come back, what then?'

'They'll be back soon.'

'They might both be killed or executed, so just think for a bit and stop being so selfish.'

'Selfish?'

'Yes. You won't handle a gun; you must leave Ireland, and all to satisfy a sick conscience! Do you think that's what Ellen wants?'

'She certainly has told you everything.'

'Ned. That soldier you piked; it surely doesn't matter now. It's no longer important. The dead should bury their dead. Just think a little about the living, the people who love you.' The old man walked angrily out of the room.

Ned dozed. There was no sign of Ellen; Grandfather had obviously got her out of the way in order to say his piece. Grandfather was wrong, he thought, about whether it was important. He could never be quite the same person again. And the old man certainly did not have rheumatisn; that was an excuse to get him to use a gun. But in other respects he might be right.

Next morning was mild, fog shrouding the trees. He took a gun and walked into the copse and shot four pheasants.

The noise and smell of the explosion worried him less than he thought. He walked for an hour or two in the fields and woods, enjoying the damp earth and listening to the familiar sounds of sheep and horses. He tramped in the sodden grass, disturbing the shining cobwebs, eating wet nuts and blackberries. He was home.

The heavy rain drilling into the ground woke him at first light. He pulled back the curtain an inch: mist and a drenching downpour. Grandfather was up, moving about downstairs in the kitchen. He slid back down the warm bed, but the movement woke Ellen.

'Listen. Shutting the world from us.'

'Ned?'

'Who else should it be?'

'Lord Camden.'

He giggled. 'I'm General Lake, and you're my prisoner.'

'Listen to that rain.'

'Poor Garret. This will finish him now. He will have to surrender.'

'Good.'

'Better this than dying in a battle.'

'Your grandfather is kind to us. He must feel shut out.'

'He was just married once upon a time. A long time ago.'

'Listen.' They heard the sound of wheels on the gravel at the front of the house.

Footsteps. Voices. 'My mother!' Ellen cried. She jumped out of bed, dressed, and hurried downstairs. Ned curled up in the warm sheets. Someone was racing along the landing. The door burst open.

'Fanny!!'

'Ned, by all that's wonderful! You're alive!'

'Of course I'm alive!'

139

'And well. You look well. Thank God you're here!'

'Come and kiss me.'

She leaned over the bed and he put his arms round her, her cold cheek wet with rain on his warm face. She burst into tears.

'I'm here; I'm alive. There's no need to be crying about it.'

She sat on the bed. 'It's not that. I've wretched news for you. The joy of finding you well put it out of my head for a second. Ned, you must get up.'

'Not till you leave, unless you want to see a stark naked man in all his pride.'

'Still as coarse as you always were! Listen, Ned. Garret and his friends have surrendered!'

'What's happened to him?' Ned sat bolt upright.

'They surrendered to General Moore. There were no trials, no court-martials, but Garret was taken to a prison in Dublin. I saw him yesterday. They're making him leave the country, and the ship—yes; it must have sailed already. It's bound for Hamburg. I have a letter here he wrote to Murtough Byrne.'

Ned took it from her. 'My dear Murtough,' he read, 'I have this day surrendered myself to General Sir John Moore, who has engaged to obtain pardon for me and permission to leave Ireland and go to reside in a foreign country. It is at the general's request I now write; he promises to obtain the same terms for you or any of the other chiefs who will immediately avail themselves of this opportunity. Yours, Garret Byrne.'

'Is Mary with him?' Ned asked.

'She was with her people in Dublin, and Dermot of course, when last I heard. I don't know if she's been allowed to go with him or not.'

140

'What can we do? Can the family at Cabinteely help us?'

'No, that's what is so dreadful. Robert Byrne died last week.'

'What!'

'A heart attack; he had high blood pressure. You remember. And he was only thirty-nine! They found him cold on the floor of his library.'

'I must get up at once.'

'Ned, there is worse to tell you. I don't know how to say it, for I want you to promise you won't try anything rash, like a rescue, or—'

'What is it?'

'Billy. He's in prison, in Wicklow. Oh, God save him, Ned! He's to be tried tomorrow. There's a power of witnesses against him. Oh, I fear the worst! He surrendered to General Lake; they say he has proved surely to be the most savage of all the English commanders. We must go there now, at once. I have a plan, no, not a rescue, but I think we could save him.'

He threw back the sheets and ran to put on his clothes. Fanny fled from the room.

Half an hour later they were galloping furiously to Wicklow, Ellen riding with them.

Billy Byrne

CHAPTER SEVEN

WICKLOW

In Wicklow they stayed with Cornelius Sinnott, whose drapery shop overlooked the main square of the town. Mr Sinnott's appearance was changed almost out of all recognition; he was able to walk only with great difficulty, and spent most of his time in an armchair in the kitchen. His wife ran the shop for him. His face was puffy and covered with bruises. He had been badly knocked about by the soldiers after they had taken him prisoner at Carlow. They had brought him back to his home town and tied him to the triangles in front of his own shop. Luckily for him they were forced to stop after about forty lashes as they were fired on by a party of rebel troops who cut him down and smuggled him away. His shop had been like Dublin Castle to the rebels, a nerve-centre of information received from spies and passed on to leaders in the Leinster Directory, and this was the reason for the flogging. Even now, with the rebellion over, except for a few tiny pockets of resistance, he was still in communication with many United Leaders. He was able to tell his visitors news they had not heard, and which was a little comfort to them, that Mary and baby Dermot had joined Garret on board the same ship, and that Garret would attempt to get in touch as soon as he arrived in Germany.

Fanny insisted, soon after they arrived, on going to the barracks to try and see General Lake. The idea of actually being face to face with this man, the most hated English soldier in Ireland, he who had massacred so many Ulstermen in 1797 and ordered thousands of rebels to be hanged or shot in Wexford only a few months previously, terrified Ned out of his wits. He would not allow Fanny to go alone, while she was adamant that Ned was not to accompany her.

'You are surely to God the most hot-tempered of men!' she cried. 'Six words in anger from you and we'll be on trial as well! You are not coming!'

'Then I shall have to use force,' he said, and dragged her into her room and locked the door. Ten minutes later he returned, and found her in floods of tears.

'Fanny. I'm sorry. But I mean it.' He kneeled down and put his arm round her. She slapped his face very hard, twice. 'You'll not be going alone,' he said, rubbing his cheek. 'Hit me again. It will make no difference,' and he put his face nearer. She raised her hand, but changed her mind. There was a long silence

'Very well,' she said at last. 'It's Billy that matters, not you or me. Just promise that when we are there you say not one word. Not one word!'

'I promise.'

But they were not allowed to see General Lake. The trial was in progress when they arrived at the barracks, and at first the guards refused to let them in. When Fanny explained who they were they were taken to the office of the general's aide-de-camp, where they were told to wait.

'Remember Ned,' Fanny said several times, 'you are not to open your mouth in any circumstances.'

'I've promised, I've promised! You're worse than a

144

parrot! Pretty Polly, pretty Polly! Not half so pretty, I'm thinking.'

'Don't be childish. We'll see; maybe a weeping woman can move a soldier's heart more easily than any argument.'

'So that is what you are planning to do. To seal Billy's fate.'

'Ned! How dare you say such a thing, at such a time?'

'I'm sorry, Fanny. It was meant to be a joke, but I guess it was feeble.'

'This is not the time nor the place for a joke!'

Footsteps; the door opened, and there stood Colonel Telford. Ned and he stared at each other for some moments. Then the Colonel held out his hand. 'I thought you would not be long in coming,' he said. 'Though I did not expect you quite like this. A romantic rescue attempt at the last moment, dashing in on horseback; that's what I imagined, and some damned fool on our side shooting you dead. Sit down.'

'Am I under arrest?' Ned asked, nervous, frightened.

'Arrest! Don't be so damned silly. I shan't forget your kind words when I was trussed up in that ice-cold tent. I was free a little sooner than you thought, eh? So I saw my wife before you could have time to be in touch with her.'

'I'm sorry, I had almost forgotten. Our own worries— Billy Byrne, too, is my brother.'

'Yes. Unfortunate. You cannot go into the court-martial; it's in secret. But you can see him this evening in his cell.'

'You mean—he's not likely to be acquitted, then?'

'No. General Lake is a hard man. Fair, of course. But hard. There seems far too much evidence against him for an acquittal.'

'What will happen to him?'

'Only General Lake knows that.'

Fanny began to weep. 'This is not your wife, I know,' said the colonel. 'I remember her quite well. Tied up as I was I could still see enough from the tent to count myself as one of your wedding guests.'

'My sister. Frances Byrne.'

'Miss Byrne. There is very little I can do. But if I can help, I will.'

Fanny dried her eyes, and, after fumbling in the bag she was carrying, produced the ancient and tattered documents that recorded the Byrne family tree. They showed, she explained, the connection between the Ballymanus family and the Byrnes of Cabinteely, and, she added, she would have gone to Robert Byrne for help. The colonel interrupted; yes, he knew Robert Byrne slightly, and had heard with sadness of his sudden death. Robert Byrne's mother, she went on, had been the sister of Earl Nugent, Lord of the Treasury to His Majesty King George II. The family tree proved it. If, and this was the point, Fanny said, her brother was convicted and had the right of appeal, this family connection might perhaps persuade General Lake to lighten the sentence.

Colonel Telford took the documents and studied them for some time.

'It isn't proof,' he said, gently.

'What do you mean?'

'General Lake might care to think it was a forgery.'

'Forgery! But you can see for yourself—'

'Miss Byrne, I believe you. But it has nothing to do with me. I will, of course, show it to General Lake, and I will use what influence I have.' He stood up. The interview was over. As he was going out he stopped, and asked 'Where are you both staying?'

146

Fanny looked nervously at Ned. 'We should not say, I think—' she began, and blushed.

'Cornelius Sinnott. You were seen arriving. Don't worry. He won't be in trouble for receiving the relatives of a United soldier on trial. He's of no further use to us. Where did you get that scar on your cheek, lad?'

'At Hacketstown, in the siege of the barracks.'

'Learn to be more discreet, Ned Byrne. If you said that to any other officer here you would probably have been marched straight to a cell. Now come back tonight at six o'clock and I will tell you what is to happen. By the way, I still have your pipe.'

Ned returned to the barracks alone. At the last moment Fanny refused to come, saying she had had a dreadful premonition that Billy was certain to be convicted. Colonel Telford, embarrassed, visibly shaken by the responsibility of having to inform him, said that Billy had been found guilty of being one of the most dangerous leaders of the United Irishmen, of murder, of conspiracy against the state, and would die by hanging, the following morning at eight o'clock. General Lake had decided the family tree was inadmissible evidence.

Fanny spent an hour in the condemned cell with Billy and returned to Sinnotts' in a state of collapse. Then it was Ned, the last member of the family allowed to see Billy.

The cell contained a bed, a chair, and a candle. For some time neither of them said much, too overcome by emotion to trust their voices. Ned sat; Billy paced up and down, hardly stopping for a moment. Guards watched them through a grille in the door. A soldier entered with a bottle of wine and glasses sent in by Ellen, then left.

Billy told Ned how they had been captured, a surprise

147

raid at dawn on their hide-out by troops of the Wicklow garrison. Most of his men had been asleep. A few were killed in a brief exchange of fire, all the rest taken to prison. Only he, the leader, had so far been tried. Other hangings were unlikely; for the rest, imprisonment, transportation, or a flogging.

'How could they think you are guilty of murder?' Ned asked.

'They said I was in charge of a party at Gorey, after the Battle of Arklow, which put Isaac Langrell to death.'

'But you were never at Gorey!'

'I know, but I could not prove it. There were several witnesses brought in to swear to it, and tortured or threatened with torture so they should tell lies. Matthew Davis of Ballinanty and John O'Toole of Greenan, both farmers' sons from good families, both swore they had seen me stick a pike into Isaac Langrell. I heard they were beaten with stones until they said they would speak and I never saw either of them before in my life. I'm told that Patrick Grant, one of the farmers who gave us food, was arrested and brought here just to swear against me, but he would not. So they flogged him to death and threw his body into the sea.'

'Such wickedness cries out for vengeance!' Ned jumped to his feet and smashed his fists into the wall. 'Oh, God! They should be ripped in pieces!'

'Ned. It makes little difference. There were plenty of counts, if anyone should believe their laws, on which they could find me guilty. I *was* a United leader, and that's enough to warrant death, even if Garret and others were treated leniently. I have killed numbers of English soldiers.'

'That was in a *war*!'

'We call it a war, but they do not! To them it's treason, an attempt to overthrow the state by its own members. It's more shocking than an attack by France or any foreign power. So: death by hanging.'

'No hope, none?'

'They offered me one way out, but I refused. If I would publicly express regret at being a United Irishman, Oliver Bond or Thomas Emmet seducing me into it, or any leader they cannot find reason to charge, and work for them, swearing against others, John Sheares or my cousin William Michael, then I could go free.'

He drank a glass of wine at one gulp, then another. Ned, who had barely sipped his, pushed it towards him. Billy laughed, a little hysterically. 'It's odd. Here am I, who was going to take Holy Orders, making myself deliberately drunk to ease my passage out of this world.'

'I will have another bottle sent, shall I?'

'Please. Though nothing will stop me from staying stone cold sober. The night before hanging will concentrate a man's mind powerfully; who was it wrote that?' He grabbed hold of Ned's lapels, and pulled him to his feet. 'What will it be like, Ned?' he whispered. 'Strangling. The longing to put my feet on the ground to ease that terrible pain in the throat. Think of it. The pain of not breathing, the slip-knot hitched under my ear—'

'Please, don't! Billy!'

Billy let him go. 'I'm sorry,' he muttered. 'There's not much else that comes into my head.' There was a long silence. 'I try to think of God and Heaven, but—it doesn't seem so clear as once it was.'

'No?'

'He exists. I have no doubts at all. What has happened to this poor Ireland would make saints doubt, but no, I'm sure. I hope I shall be saved. I am allowed a priest to hear my confession and give me Communion; my Lord and my God

149

in me as I go out to die. That is comfort, a great comfort, and the priest will be here as soon as your hour is up and stay with me till the end. No, it's not that.' He knelt down, his head in Ned's lap. 'I'm terrified. That's all. I shall shit my breeches with terror. Help me.'

Ned stroked his hair, then said, 'I'm so helpless with words! No use! No use at all!'

'Biddy Doyle spoke out against me.'

'Who?'

'That girl, Ned. You won't have forgotten.'

'My fault—'

'No, not your fault.' He sprang up, and began pacing up and down again. 'She would surely have been coaxed into it anyway. Though it would not have mattered if she had not been brought in at all; she made little difference to verdict or sentence.'

'But, what, what did she say?'

'Oh, a pack of lies! She had seen me kill such and such, and so and so. That I had allowed parties of rebel soldiers to have their way with her. Would I do the like of that?'

'Billy, Billy, I'm so sorry, I can't—'

'Ned, it is not your fault!! Be quiet!!' He seized Ned by the hair and shook him. 'I just hope you will never go to such a woman!'

'I'm married, Billy. Did you not know?'

Billy released him. 'Of course. Forgive me. My young brother is married and I . . . That such a thing should be put from my mind.' He wiped his face with his hands; he was sweating, though the night was very cold and the cell unheated. He swallowed some more wine. 'How is Ellen?'

'Well enough. None of us, at the moment, are ourselves.'

'No. I hope, Ned, you saw a priest before you were married. I mean, for confession.'

'I did not.'

'Ned!'

'I was not ready.'

'Such a step as marriage needs prayer. I wish I had been a priest. I would like to have married the pair of you.'

'I hardly pray at all now. It's six months since I last went to the sacraments.'

'You should go. Often. Are you losing the Faith?'

'No. But I think a man should go to Communion when he needs to, not as a habit.'

'You should not lose the habit of prayer. I'm praying all the time, especially when I see the image of that rope in front of my eyes. I should be in darkness and hopeless despair otherwise. Isn't despair the most terrible thing that can happen to a man?'

'I know, I know!'

'It's not the same as terror. I think I can say I have never known despair.'

'I have. When I was in prison. I hated myself and everyone else, fighting other young men for a scrap of potato skin, not caring if they should starve.'

'Ned, I did not know.'

'I don't want to talk about it. It's over now, lost in the past.'

'Ned. Do go to a priest.'

'It's scarcely possible, Billy, to believe that with what you are facing you can worry about another man's soul.'

'Is it vanity in me?'

'No. Goodness.'

'Is it? The habit of the priestly mind, more likely. I don't know if that is goodness or not.' He finished the wine, staggering slightly. 'Do you still wear the cross Ellen gave you?'

'No. I lost it. No, it's a lie; I threw it away in despair.'

'I am wearing one round my neck. I want you to have it. It's the twin of the other; they're both very old. They belonged to our great-grandparents and one came to us, one to Ellen's father. Please take it.' He lowered his head, and Ned moved to unfasten the chain on which it hung, but overwhelmed by the tragedy of it all, he clasped his brother in his arms and kissed him passionately, on his eyes and lips and hair.

'Billy, I can't bear it! I love you so much!'

Billy, with a great effort of will, pulled Ned's arms away, and said, unsteadily, 'It's little help now.' He unfastened the chain himself and gave it to Ned.

The key turned in the lock, and the priest came in.

'Goodbye, Ned.'

'I can't say it, my throat is too full! I—'

'Please pray again, Ned. I need those prayers.'

Ned went into an alehouse in a poor quarter of the town. He was tense and shaking after his hour with Billy and could not face the idea of returning at once to Sinnotts'. He was incapable of dealing with his own emotions, let alone those of Ellen or Fanny. Alcohol seemed as necessary for the moment as it was for Billy.

The tavern was full of labourers, all discussing one topic, for the news of Billy's trial and death sentence had been deliberately leaked out by the authorities, in order to instil fear in the people. They looked at Ned suspiciously, but when he mentioned who he was he became the focus of attention, and did not need to buy himself a drink all the time he was there. Several voices wanted to know how Billy was, calm, or defiant or frightened; was there any chance of a reprieve?

'No chance, no chance,' Ned muttered. 'Please, I can't talk of it.'

'Leave him be! Don't upset him now! Let him alone!' came several voices.

A man in the corner by the fire began singing quietly, one of the many songs the events of that year had already inspired, a melancholy song of defeat as almost all of them were. By the end of the verse everyone except Ned had joined in.

'I met with Napper Tandy and he took me by the
hand,
Saying, how is old Ireland? and how does she stand?
She's the most distressful country that ever yet was
seen;
They are hanging men and women for wearing of
the green!
O wearing of the green, O wearing of the green,
My native land, I cannot stand, for wearing of the
green!'

'You should not sing that!' said the landlady, before they could start another verse.

'Why not, why not?'

'You don't know who might be listening. Besides, you're upsetting the lad.' She poured another whiskey and pushed it to Ned. 'It's on the house, it is, and any more yourself should be wanting.'

'What are we doing to stop it all?' cried one of the drinkers. 'We should all be out there in the morning with our pikes to stop it!'

'We should! We should!'

'Pikes? What pikes? They've all been broken or burnt.'

153

'No they have not. There's plenty hidden away for another year.'

'We'll not let such a man be strangled like a chicken!'

'The finest gentleman I ever met. Dwyer, Holt, Perry, compared with him they're nothing. Why, when we were at Carlow did you know he was spending an hour seeing the Protestant minister was properly cared for in hospital, and him not thinking of his own bad wounds! The *Protestant* minister! That's the man Billy Byrne was.'

'You were never at Carlow.'

'Oh yes I was, Pat Sewell. I could tell you a story about your brother if I so cared, may the good Lord rot him.'

'Oh what? Tell us, tell us.'

'Why, at the siege of Ross he was sat behind a barrel of port and never fired a blessed shot.'

'Lies, all lies, Dan Cronin!'

'Yes he did so. He came out every while and was asking "How goes the day, boys?" And back he would hide when another bullet shaved past him.'

Pat Sewell stalked out in anger, but everyone else laughed. Ned swallowed another whiskey, and began to feel light-headed. He supported himself against the counter. Someone began another song.

'At the siege of Ross did my father fall
And at Gorey my loving brothers all,
I alone am left of my name and race,
I will go to Wexford and take their place.'

'There's many like that. There's the poor widow of Rathnew, Widow Galvin, d'you know her? Her man was shot at her door in front of her eyes. A little place it is, but they had some corn and a few pigs, and lived. All her five sons died at Arklow, or Enniscorthy, or the Lord knows

154

where. And the daughters followed the rebels and now they're racked with disease, they say.'

'Ireland! Ireland!'

'It was early, early in the spring
When small birds tune, and thrushes sing,
Changing their note from tree to tree
And the song they sang was old Ireland free.'

'They're all gone now. The finest of the men and the best of the women. All gone.'

'What is it you say, they're all gone? May the Lord strike you dead! Down, down, croppies, lie down, the Orangemen sing, but I still see many croppies in Wicklow, town and county.'

'But the gold sun of Freedom grew darkened at Ross,
And it set by the Slaney's red waves;
And poor Wexford, stripped naked, hung high on a
                                                    cross,
And her heart pierced by traitors and slaves!'

'Sure it is we should be in that barracks pulling him out and not standing here, for we're not yet singing at his wake! What say you?'

'We haven't a chance.'

'I've more than half a mind,' said Ned. 'Just give me a musket.'

'Aye, and half a dozen cannon you'll be needing too.'

'We should wait till morning. We should fire on them from the roof-tops, just as we did when they tied Con Sinnott to the triangles. He would surely get away in the noise and fuss.'

'Drive in the cows. A stampede, like Ross.'

'Useless. They'd hang us all.'

'We've bled all we can stand.'

'Where is the courage of you all? Come, who's willing to join a rescue-party in the morning?'

'Yes, we are, I am, we'll be there!' Most of the men agreed.

' "The Boys will all be there, with their pikes in good repair",' the singer began, ' "And Lord Edward will be there—".' But he broke off as the door was flung open, and an officer from the barracks came in. A patrol of armed soldiers stood just outside on the pavement.

'Closing time,' he said, when all the voices had died away.

'But it's not yet half past nine!' protested the landlady.

'Orders from General Lake. All spirit shops and ale houses to be closed at nine o'clock tonight. It's quarter past now. Come on, all of you, get out.'

The drinkers began to shuffle out into the street, their courage and dreams of a rescue evaporating immediately.

'Riot prevention,' said the officer to the landlady. 'There's to be a hanging in the morning, and we don't want people to get the wrong ideas in their heads. I'll have a whiskey, please.'

'We're closed.'

The officer smiled. 'It's on the house,' he said.

Ned walked unsteadily across the square. It was full of men, some holding torches, others hammering and sawing wood. A large number of troops stood by, watching. The workmen were building a scaffold.

Ellen was in bed, but not asleep. 'You smell like a Dublin brewery,' she said, disgusted. 'Where have you been?'

'With friends. They're plotting a rescue in the morning.' He tried to put his arms round her, but she pushed him away.

'A rescue! Oh no, you do not, Ned Byrne, brother or not!'

'Who's to stop me?'

'I will.'

Ned laughed for the first time that day.

Though he thought he would not he slept, and slept well. He woke to find everyone else had been up for some time. It was half past seven. Fanny was silent, pale and red-eyed, standing at the window. Ned put his arm round her and looked down on the square. It was raining, but already a large crowd had assembled. They were silent and orderly, just waiting. In the centre was the hastily erected gallows, its rope dangling.

'I'm going out,' said Ned.

'Would you go down to the cellar first?' Ellen asked. 'Mr. Sinnott wants some bales of cloth brought up for the shop. He's too weak to do it himself, and they're too heavy for his wife.'

Unsuspecting, Ned climbed down into the cellar, holding a candle to light the way. The trap-door slammed behind him and was bolted. He heaved at it with all his strength and the bolt began to give. But something heavy was being pushed over it; he heard Ellen's voice and Mrs Sinnott's, and a lot of banging; it sounded like the sofa from the kitchen being pushed on top, and several heavy boxes.

'Let me out! Let me out! Ellen, I will murder you for this!'

He heaved and pushed with his shoulders and arms and legs, banged at the door with his fists and his head till the blood came, and went on uselessly kicking and smashing at the wood in a blind senseless rage. He accidentally knocked the candle over and he was in total darkness.

He only stopped when he heard the furniture being moved away. The bolt slipped back, and Ellen pulled up the trap-door as quickly as she could, stepping away rapidly,

157

for fear he would charge out like a wild animal. But he did not.

'Ellen! Come here!'

Terrified, she came slowly down the steps into the darkness. He picked her up and nearly smashed her into the wall. She screamed with fright, and he relaxed; she fell on to a bale of cloth and he subsided on top of her.

'Ellen, my darling, my Ellen, how could you do that to me?' And he covered her in kisses, and broke down and sobbed his heart out.

They went out into the square. Ned had one arm round Ellen, one round Fanny. Both women wept unrestrainedly. The crowd had all gone; the square was deserted, except for Billy. Ned gazed at the poor face of his brother, purple and distorted with suffering. The rain streamed down. The wind moved the body gently; it was like a heavy life-size doll, left by a child out in the wet.

Later they went to the barracks to ask what was to happen to the body. They were given permission to take him where and when they saw fit; and on the next day Billy was buried. The town came to a standstill for the funeral. Shops shut for the day. Alehouses were empty. Hundreds of people stood silent and bare-headed in the rain as the coffin was taken from Sinnotts'. They filled the church for the service, and thronged the graveyard for the burial.

The next morning Ned, Ellen and Fanny left for Ballymanus.

CHAPTER EIGHT

DUBLIN

For several months their spirits were very low. They heard from Garret, just after Christmas; a long letter, with all the details of how and why he had surrendered, the voyage to Germany, how appalled he was to hear what had happened to Billy. He and Mary were planning to live in France; a distant cousin, Miles Byrne of Monaseed, had settled in Paris, having been forced, like Garret, to flee the country after the rebellion. He had suggested that they shared a house together.

Ned was now truly the master of Ballymanus. He busied himself learning all the things that had formerly been left to Garret, accounts, book-keeping, what was a fair price to pay for pigs and sheep. The big armchair in the kitchen was his; the bedroom Garret and Mary had used, and which his parents and grandparents had slept in before them, was now permanently his and Ellen's. The household ran to his orders and his timetable. He grew his beard again, as Ellen was still curious to see what he had looked like at Tullow.

Grandfather never fully recovered from the shock of Billy's death, and once he knew that Ned was running things wisely, he appeared to lose the last traces of energy that had helped him live through the events of that year. The rebuilding of the house he seemed to regard as his last useful service to his family. He became suddenly fragile and ancient, and in the bad weather of the early months of 1799, he died peacefully in his sleep, a few days before his eighty-fifth birthday. He was buried in the family vault in the village churchyard.

Mrs Kennedy still lived in the cottage. After Grand-father's death she hinted to Fanny on several occasions that it would be more politic if the young couple could now be left on their own in the house, and that Fanny perhaps might move to Cabinteely, or, if that was too far, the cottage had plenty of spare room, and it was lonely sometimes living on one's own, though she was saying nothing against Ellen and Ned who were kindness itself and everything a fond daughter and devoted son-in-law could be. Fanny wondered if she was not perhaps right. One day she broached the subject with Ned, who flatly refused to entertain the idea of her moving, unless she really hated living with them. 'If I should see you packing,' he said, 'I shall bolt you in the cellar just as Ellen did to me. Only I shall keep you there longer.'

'I should know better how to get out!'

'Just try if you don't believe me. Just try. But it's good, sister, to see you smile again.'

Fanny stayed, pleased that they really wanted her. She had never lived anywhere else in her life, knew nobody much outside the family; her whole satisfaction was to do what her adored Ned wished for.

One night when they were in bed, Ellen said 'I think we shall soon be having a child born in this house.' Ned put his hand on her. 'There's no kicking to feel yet, and you're more ignorant than you think! It's lower down! I'm weeks late now, and I can't bear, all of a sudden, the taste of coffee and food at breakfast. And the way you eat meat like a wolf.'

'I've been hoping for months that you would be saying this!'

'Have you? I thought you didn't care for babies.'

'I've changed. It's Dermot you're thinking of; *he's* not *my* son.'

'Fanny will be pleased.'

Ned was delighted with the news. 'We'll tell her in the morning. Oh, she will be dancing! And she'll spoil him utterly!'

'Him?'

'Of course.'

'Garret Byrne.'

'No, not Garret. We have to break the tradition. Billy Byrne.'

'Yes.'

He was silent for a while, then he said 'Me, a father! When will he be born? November?'

'Should be. We'll be a few months over twenty. How will we manage, I wonder?'

'We've all lived a lifetime since that day the soldiers came here.'

'I can feel your scars still.'

'I've forgotten them.'

'Two lashes,' Ellen said. 'And they will mar you for ever.'

'Do you like my beard?'

'Yes. Though you don't look much like the Ned Byrne I first knew. You've changed.'

'I'm the green tree of liberty. My arms are its boughs.'

'Where did it first grow?'

'Not in America. Here in Ireland.'

'Where did it bud?'

He laughed. 'Not in France. When I first knew I loved you.'

'Where are you going to plant it?'

'I could give you a coarse answer! But it's planted already, months back, here in this bed at Ballymanus. We shall start a new forest.'

But it did not happen. The English, as usual, had the last word; on the day following this conversation Ned received a letter from the magistrates in Wicklow, ordering him to present himself at the court in a week's time. Nothing in the letter suggested why he was required to go there; 'I can't imagine what it can be about,' he said several times to Ellen. 'We've done nothing wrong, broken no laws. Not since the rebellion, that is, and I should have thought that matter was closed by now.'

'Maybe it isn't.'

'We shall see. One of us hanged, another in exile: what more can they want?'

'That's all very well. Garret and Billy have been punished; you escaped scot free.'

'I? Scot free? One battle, that's all I saw of the fighting, and it led to months in prison. Have you forgotten?'

'No.'

'Anyway, this letter isn't a warrant; no-one has come to arrest me. Oh . . . it's probably some minor legal point. Something to do with Grandfather's will.'

'As you said: we shall see.'

He had guessed right in that he was not to be charged with any offence; the presiding magistrate in fact received him very politely at the court-house. When they had exchanged a number of civilities about the weather, and established that

164

Ned had had an easy journey from Ballymanus to Wicklow, the magistrate said, looking at a document he held in his hand, 'Now the purpose of this visit.'

'Yes,' Ned answered. 'What is the purpose? I'm a farmer and I have work to do; I hope it will not take long.'

'You farm the land at Ballymanus?'

'Of course. There is no-one else to do it. Now.'

'And you live in the house?'

'Naturally.'

'And who else lives there?'

'My wife and my sister. Why all these questions? My family has owned Ballymanus for a century. Since January the thirteenth, 1700, to be precise. I have documents to prove it.'

The magistrate took off his glasses. 'It once belonged to your brother Garret, did it not?'

'Yes.' And Billy lived there too, Ned thought. Earlier, when he was crossing the square to the court-house, he had stood for a few moments, bareheaded and bowed, trying to pray, on the spot where Billy had been hanged.

'Then you have no legal right to be there.'

Ned was astounded. 'No legal right! What nonsense is this?'

'Your brother was deeply involved with the United Irishmen, one of their military leaders, commander-in-chief of their forces at the Battle of Hacketstown, and a delegate to the Leinster Directory.'

'And now he's in exile for his pains, living out the rest of his life in a foreign country.'

'Yes. The property of all such people has been confiscated by the British crown.'

'What!!'

'I have instructions here from the authorities in Dublin

165

ordering you and your dependents to leave Ballymanus within five days.'

Ned was too flabbergasted to speak. His first impulse was to seize the magistrate by the throat and strangle him, but that was not likely to help much: he stood amazed, clenching and unclenching his fists, his mouth open. 'And if I refuse to be ejected?' he said at last.

'Resisting eviction? You could be put in jail. As would your wife and your sister if they continued to stay there. It would go hard against you. We could re-open old wounds; your part in last year's disturbances has never been properly examined. It's rumoured that you were responsible for the death of General Dundas' son.'

'But that was in a war!'

'War? You call it a war?' The magistrate shook his head. 'I should leave quietly if I were you.'

'But . . . we . . . we have nowhere to go!'

'Have you any children?'

'None as yet.'

'Then that is one less worry for you.'

'My wife is pregnant.'

'Is she? Unfortunate.'

'Unfortunate! Is that all you can say? Nowhere to go . . . no money . . .' He ran his hands through his hair several times. 'Are we allowed to take our furniture, our farm implements, all our goods and chattels?'

'According to the law, everything at Ballymanus right down to the last knife and fork is your brother's property.'

Ned lost his temper. 'I'll see the house burned to a cinder first! I'll lock us all in and shoot every stranger who comes near the gate! And I'd kill my sister and my wife and myself before I'd allow another owner to set foot in the place!' He walked out, slamming the door so hard that a picture fell

166

off the wall. He heard the glass smash as it hit the floor.

He visited several taverns and got himself rather drunk before he rode home. So much for planting a new forest, he thought; so much for his vision of new generations of Byrnes living at Ballymanus, himself as head of the family, the patriarch: what was this green tree of liberty? A withered deformed growth, a seed that had fallen among stones and died, starved of light and water and air.

Fanny and Ellen were appalled by the news, but much more inclined than he was to accept their fate and think of practical things they could do. 'We're not leaving!' Ned shouted again and again. 'We are *not* leaving! We'll barricade ourselves in and shoot it out!' They told him not to be so silly, but to try and think of what they could do to lessen their misfortune.

'The wisest course of action,' Fanny said, 'is to start packing at once. Take everything we can; strip the rooms bare tomorrow and the day after, so that whoever comes to take possession on Tuesday finds nothing left but an empty shell. We can store most of the furniture at your mother's, Ellen; the rest with our friends. And we'll leave as soon as the house is empty.'

'Where shall we go?' Ellen asked.

'To Dublin.' Fanny surprised herself, making such a decision, but it was clear that they would get no sense out of Ned at the moment and something had to be done. 'We'll go to Mary's family,' she said.

'We'll do nothing of the sort!' Ned growled. 'And not one chair, not one dinner-plate is to be moved out of this house without my permission!' He left the room.

'Where are you going?'

'To find some whiskey. I'm going to drink myself unconscious!'

167

Ellen went after him. She found him in the stables, sitting in the straw, staring at nothing. 'Ellen . . . Ellen!' He put his arms round her. 'What are we going to do?'

'I don't know, Ned. I don't know. But remember . . . there's a child coming.'

'What work can I do? I can manage a farm; nothing else. I'll never be a soldier again. Never!'

'You're young. And strong.'

'Learn a trade. Me? A Byrne of Ballymanus learning a trade! But what else am I fit for? I've little skill for any profession.'

'There'll be something.'

'Ned Byrne the blacksmith!' He laughed bitterly.

'You have the build for it. They're all great hairy men; you . . . when I see you in bed you look from top to toe like a human ape.'

'My children, growing up in poverty in Dublin. Among thieves and pimps and whores!' It was a cry of pain, from deep inside. '*No*!!'

'Come into the house; we'll discuss it all in the morning.' He allowed himself to be led away. Fanny was already packing the china and glass into boxes, and did not stop when she saw him. He said nothing, just looked at her with eyes full of misery.

Fanny was up early, sending for friends and neighbours; and all next day from early morning till late afternoon, carts loaded with furniture and the family's personal belongings left for various houses in the district where barns and sheds were large enough and dry enough to store their possessions. Ned watched it all in a curiously dream-like detached manner as if it was not really happening, as if he would wake up at any moment and find things restored to normality. He walked about the farm, not knowing what he was doing nor why. At least Grandfather and Billy did not live to see this, he said to himself, and Garret, hundreds of miles away in France, was ignorant of what was going on. Perhaps they could go to Paris and join his brother: it might, in the long run, be a good idea; but Fanny's scheme, of staying with Mary's family in Dublin, would do for the moment. To return to Cabinteely was something they had ruled out; since Robert Byrne's death there could be no help in that quarter, for his wife had left for England and the house was shut up, in the process of being sold. Ned wondered what right of appeal he had against the decision to confiscate Ballymanus; he considered returning to Wicklow with the two women and pleading his case—humbly and pathetically if necessary— but it undoubtedly would be futile, as well as distressing and humiliating. He knew that many others who had been active in the rebellion had lost their property in a similar manner; he had been foolish and blind not to think he would suffer too. But he had thought, since taking over the running of the farm, that he was one of the lucky few to escape. General Moore's leniency to Garret—the general was supposed to have said that if he had been Irish he would have been a rebel—and his own flight from Glenmalure, which meant that he was not obliged to surrender to the English troops and have his own role questioned, had lulled him into a sense of completely false security.

He leaned on the gate, remembering that day a year ago, when he and Billy had stood there watching Cornelius Sinnott ride pell-mell up the road from Aughrim, the day when the news had come of the arrest of all the leaders at Oliver Bond's: how young and innocent, how lacking in knowledge of the ways of the world the two of them had been then! How absurd to think that a few weeks' gentle fighting, with perhaps a not too painful wound for Fanny or Ellen to nurse and heroic stories at the fireside to pass on to the next generation, would be the result of that bloody summer! What was it Mary had said? 'A bloody summer, Ireland's fall, no husband, and chaos for us all.' Now Billy was dead. And he—he had killed several people; God only knew how many: he had married, conceived a child, learned how to run a farm, seen the full inhuman savagery of men in battle and in prison. All in twelve months. He was old now in experience, years beyond his age: and not yet twenty.

He was broken from his thoughts by the sound of horses on the road. He looked up: a party of soldiers. His first reaction was nervousness; he was without a weapon to defend himself. But that was silly; it was peace now, not war. A kind of peace: the triangles had been put away, and no news came of pillage, arson, rape, massacres. The grip of English authority on Irish life had never been stronger.

The soldiers stopped. Ned recognized the leader, Matthew Gowan, now a captain in the Wicklow Yeomen Cavalry. 'I just thought I'd tell you,' he said, 'that the regiment will be here in force on Tuesday to supervise the eviction ceremonies.'

Ned walked away, seething with anger. Yes, Fanny had been right to start packing at once. He was glad, however, that there were no laden carts on the road or outside the house at that moment; the soldiers would certainly make trouble if the family was seen moving its property. He stood behind one of the monkey-puzzle trees and watched: if he had his musket with him he could pick off Matthew with no more difficulty than winging a pheasant. How easily old enemies revived the instinct to shoot and kill!

By noon on the following day the house was empty. So were the out-buildings: the farm implements, the livestock, the straw and hay, everything that could be taken had gone. Neighbours had come during the night and removed it all. Ned had sold most of it at knock-down prices to grateful friends and acquaintances; he obtained only a fraction of its total worth, but at least it gave the family sufficient money to live on for a while. The rooms in the house, now bare, echoed forlornly and looked damp and cheerless. He stood in his bedroom. He had been born here; one act of love-making in this room had created him, just as he and Ellen, years afterwards, had started another life on its progress into the world. His mother had died here on a grey December afternoon, snow fluttering against the windows. So much pleasure and pain, so much significance: the extraordinary mysterious unfathomable meaning of it all.

In what had been the drawing room, Fanny said 'Garret behind his desk.'

'Grandfather and his documents,' Ned answered.

She ran a finger along the dust on the mantelpiece. 'I remember a Sunday morning when I was seven, just sitting here.'

'What were you doing?'

'Nothing. Just watching the May sunshine stream through the windows. Billy came in and said "What would you like for breakfast?"'

'There's a new existence to think of,' Ellen said. 'For all of us.'

'Let's go.'

They took their places on the cart, Ellen and Ned at the front, Fanny in the back with the luggage. Ned thought of the wet evening after the fire when they had started on their journey to Cabinteely. The green bough, the green tree of liberty! Twice he had tried to plant his own green tree and twice he had failed; trusting in a place and a vision of a new dynasty of Byrnes at Ballymanus, trusting in a dream of his country's freedom that had been rocked to nightmare. There was no such thing as the green bough of liberty, not for him nor for any Irishman of his generation; it was a wraith, a shadow only, a faint hope to be kept alive in the heart. Perhaps for his and Garret's descendants, their great-great-great-grandchildren, there would be such a reality, scattered wherever they might be, in France or America, even in England. Somehow, some time in the future, two hundred years hence maybe, someone would see that justice would be done.

> She's the most distressful country that ever yet was seen;
> They are hanging men and women for wearing of the green,
> O wearing of the green, O wearing of the green,
> My native land, I cannot stand, for wearing of the green!

They reached the cross-roads, and turned into the valley, the way that led through Aughrim. Ballymanus disappeared from sight.

POSTSCRIPT

The 1798 rebellion was undoubtedly the most serious threat the English rulers of Ireland had ever faced, and had it succeeded history might have been very different. The sectarian divisions that have bedevilled the country in modern times might never have occurred, for the United Irishmen respected each other's religion, and Ulster was, curiously, a hotbed of rebels wishing to sever the English connection. The fighting there in 1798 was second in scope and intensity only to County Wexford.

More than thirty thousand men, women, and children died in the rebellion. We do not hear much of it in history lessons in English schools, though Thomas Pakenham, in his book, *THE YEAR OF LIBERTY*, calls it 'the most violent and tragic event in Irish history between the Jacobite wars and the Great Famine', and William Lecky, in his *HISTORY OF IRELAND IN THE EIGHTEENTH CENTURY*, says it was 'a scene of horrors hardly surpassed in the modern history of Europe.' Beside it, the sufferings of modern Ulster, or the period 1916–1923, pale into insignificance. It was the last hope for a totally united Ireland, and its failure, Pakenham suggests, has left 'a legacy of violence and hatred that has persisted to the present day.' One of the members of the government of the time, Lord Wycombe, referred to it as 'an union of English imbecility with Irish ferocity,' and I think that is a fair comment.

175

The Byrne family really existed. Billy was in fact hanged on September 26th, 1799 at Wicklow. Ned married twice, his first wife dying in 1802. He had seven children and died in 1824. Garret, my great-great-great-grandfather, died in Paris in 1832 and was buried at Montparnasse. The letter quoted in Chapter Six was actually written by him. His wife Mary died in Dublin in 1834. Fanny never married. She died at Dublin in 1831.

I have taken liberties with history in a number of respects. Various events mentioned in this story occurred at dates earlier or later in 1798 than I have said; the rebel camp at Hacketstown is borrowed from the scene at Vinegar Hill in County Wexford; the Byrnes of Ballymanus were related to the Cabinteely family much more distantly than I have suggested. The characters and the behaviour of all the people in this story are, of course, purely fictional.

It is perhaps fitting to allow Miles Byrne of Monaseed, a cousin of Garret, Billy, Fanny and Ned, to have the last word. He, too, fought in the rebellion and wrote a very interesting account of it in his *MEMOIRS*, which were published in Paris in 1863. 'Edward Byrne, or "Little Ned" as we used to call him, though he was six feet high, because he was the last of the brothers, was brother to Garret Byrne of Ballymanus, and to the ever-to-be-lamented William Byrne who was executed at Wicklow, and to whose sister Fanny Lord Cornwallis had promised a reprieve; but this cold-hearted inhuman man did not keep his promise. He allowed the unhappy young lady to repair to Wicklow to weep over the cold remains of her unhappy brother, whose only crime was having saved the lives of many prisoners at the risk of his own; his innocence became proverbial ever after through the country; when anyone was going to be tried, the people would cry out "Oh! surely that man is as innocent as poor Billy Byrne!"'